FORWARD

I always wanted to write an autobiography about my life growing up as a graffiti artist in North Hollywood, California in the eighties. It was a harrowing time, height of the L.A. gang wars, crime was rampant, danger around every corner. What kept me from putting pen to paper over these many years is the nature of my experiences; many were so truly unbelievable they would be taken as lies.

Eventually after years of being plagued by my memories I chose to write a fictional account in a scripted form for a possible TV series. It tells the story of Den, a teenage graffiti artist in Venice Beach, California who has a deeply troubled life and incredibly gifted talent, both of which haunt him. He meets an equally troubled girl while painting in Venice, only she is from Bel Air, which may as well be on the moon as far as Den is concerned. Fall in love they do, this opens a trap-door landing them in a world of shit.

Much of the essence of this story is born from truth, although my life experience was in some ways far crazier than the character I created, the universe in which we both exist is very much the same. Bringing the script into a novel format was challenging, but I just wanted to share it, I am compelled to share it.

Life is a confusing and perplexing psychological mind-fucker at times, especially when you have nothing to offer society except your expression. I have been blessed these years to live a wholly artistic life-experience, but I often think what would have become of me had I not fell into professional acting at such a ripe age. The success garnered afforded me the ability to explore life exactly how I wanted to, even the madness of it all. One never-ending constant which has followed me through it all is my love of graffiti art; this book is a culmination of many years spent fruitlessly pursing graffiti and street art, putting so much time and energy into something that has never returned the favor.

I don't paint and stencil, or paste-up for fame or fortune, I do it to leave a piece of me behind where before there was nothing at all, and so it is with this first novel that I do the same thing; leave a piece of me behind.

Corin Nemec

planetstreet.com

VENICE HIGH

Written

by

Corin Nemec

ISBN #: 978-1-387-53065-6

CHAPTER INDEX

"They wander in darkness seeking light, failing to realize that the light is in the heart of the darkness"

Manly P. Hall

CHAPTER ONE — CATCHING HEAVENS

STREETS OF VENICE, CALIFORNIA — NIGHT

Crossbeams of colored lights refract off damp asphalt from a recent rain, three in the morning and streets of Venice, California are empty as a beggar's coin-purse. In a city as populated as Los Angeles one would expect people out at all hours, but after two forty-five AM, everywhere in L.A. is a ghost town.

1830's Venice Beach, California was called *La Ballona* and was not California at all but Mexico, which really wasn't that long ago if you think about it. It became part of these United States in the late 1840's, fifty years later the land was purchased by a Tobacco tycoon named Abbot Kinney to build a seaside resort town. Mr. Kinney dug the canals to give it the feel of his favorite place in Italy, then built up the infrastructure and founded the City of Venice in the early 1900's.

In the mid 1920's the City of Venice was annexed by the City of Los Angeles, which quickly ignored it, letting it slowly sink back into the marshland it was drained from, actively filling in many of the famed canals that gave it its' namesake to lay more roads. Mostly it was seen as a financial black-hole for Los Angeles, so they limited their monetary involvement as much as possible.

By the 1950's it was kindly regarded as *"Slum by the Sea"*, populated predominantly by low-wage earners, vagabonds, poor immigrants, and a lot of minorities. Because of the barbarous environment Venice became a hotbed for the counterculture scene exploding in America after WWII, quartering a wave of bikers, hippies, gangsters, artists, writers, and plenty of bums.

By the eighties the *Slum by the Sea* had graduated to being called *Ghetto by the Sea*, which is way classier if you ask me. These days there are not many cheap places left to live in Venice, but poor folk still manage to call it home.

Footsteps slap down the sidewalk as three teenagers in dark clothes and backpacks duck into an alley.

BACK ALLEY - NIGHT

Water drips from pipes running up the back of a four story brick building, landing with a hollow plop in dirty puddles below. Rubber soles squeak on the sides of a graffiti covered trash-bin as a *Vans* high-top sneaker, covered in paint with a pinky toe peeking out from a tear in the canvas, steps quietly on the bin's metal lid.

The mysterious figure reaches for a fire ladder hanging down from above, distracted by the sound of loud splashing. He looks down at his best-friend Blast, a *baby-faced* Mexican teen with a stout figure actively pissing against the brick wall.

DEN

Really, Blast?! Now?

Looking down from above is Den, the quintessential *west coast kid*, salty blonde locks messy and long, emerald green eyes peering from beneath a saggy hoodie, his youthful streamlined features mask the ugliness he feels inside.

Blast whispers loudly—

                    BLAST
          Bro, my nerves, man.

Both are sixteen, but Den is fit and athletic, quickly pulling himself up the ladder as the third hooded youth hops up behind him, nearly slipping from the trash-bin.

Blast reaches over and steadies him.

                    CASE
          That better not be the hand you pissed
                    with, cuz.

Case is a light skinned mulatto, nineteen years old with scruffy facial hair and deep scar carved across his forehead. He was best friends with Den's older brother but only hangs with Den now.

                    BLAST
          I'm gonna need help up to that ladder,
                    Case.

Blast sees Den already climbing up a thin work ladder reaching near fifty feet from the rooftop of the building to a massive commercial billboard floating overhead.

                    BLAST
          Den, wait up! Not cool, man.

Blast zips up his over-sized baggy black *Dickies* work-pants, climbing the trash-bin like a *gorilla on a truck-tire*, girth causes groans from the metal as he achingly hoists himself up, nearly knocking Case off.

BLAST

Sorry, homie.

Blast can barely reach the ladder above, struggling against gravity he moans, frustrated. Case gives him a comical and truly difficult boost up to the ladder—

CASE

Lose some weight, fool...

BLAST

I've lost tons, dude.

CASE

I think you found it again.

Blast finally has a grip and climbs to the roof, followed quickly by Case, who is very strong and agile.

ROOFTOP - NIGHT

From the roof it's easy to see eight blocks in each direction of Lincoln Boulevard. Eerily quiet at this hour every movement seems to echo forever. Case, with cat-like moves, scurries over an industrial air-conditioning unit then hops to a ladder that dangles out over the street.

Case climbs the billboard ladder as it stretches into the night, ending at a massive commercial billboard shining down from above like a glittering angel with *"Drink Coca-Cola"* across her chest.

                              BLAST
                      Fuck heights, homie.

   Blast hunkers down on the roof, going no
further. He pulls a *Twix* candy-bar and walkie-
talkie out of his bag, staring intently at the
sprawling city before him.

   He ravenously tears open the Twix wrapper
with his teeth, insatiable hunger never
satisfied.

BILLBOARD - NIGHT

   High above the rooftop Case reaches a narrow
platform where Den slips on black rubber
gloves like a professional cat-burglar, wind
whipping around them, swaying the iron
structure with a low, steal groan. There is
nothing to keep them from falling off this
thing, one wrong move, one slip, one step back
and its certain death.

                              CASE
                Hella creepy out tonight, Den.

                              DEN
             Only thing creepy out is you, Case.

   The night is blustery, electricity hums low
as seventy feet in the clouds two teens seek
fame and glory by catching *Heavens*; Heavens is
slang in the graffiti culture for tagging
anything high above the ground.

   Removing their backpacks, both take out
heavy black panels of cloth, draping them over
the billboard lights, plunging all into
darkness. Den looks between his legs, thin
aluminum platform between him and immortality.

City lights bath Den and Case in a disco-pink wash; they take cans of *Ironlak* spray-paint from their backpacks, putting *yellow-universal tips* on them and paint over the lower portion of the massive *Coca-Cola* advertisement.

Den and Case bomb it; bombing being a useful term to describe illegally painting some unsuspecting public space. Differing angles of *Roark-black* and *Aspen-white* lines stretch across their canvas, filling in negative spaces with an *Astro-cap* on a can of vibrant *Soviet-red*, fat, flaring lines quickly covering *Coca-Cola* with their own words in the *exact same font*; leaving part of the ad that reads *Drink*.

ROOFTOP – SAME TIME

Blast finishes his *Twix* and drops the wrapper off the roof. As it flutters toward the ground a Police Car appears up the street driving in his direction. He triggers his walkie, alerting his friends to the danger—

BLAST

One-time-one-time-one-time.

One-time means cops because it only takes *one-time* to throw you in jail *forever*.

BILLBOARD – SAME TIME

High upon the narrow scaffolds, Den and Case hear Blast's voice whispering from their walkie-talkie. They lay down upon the rafter as Cops pass slowly below.

The cruiser pulls to a stop at the corner, officer in the driver's seat hidden by dark

shadows, the police lights are activated
sending sherbet beams in all directions, siren
kicks on and the cop car speeds away.

Case and Den get up, returning to painting—

CASE

Piggies can't fly, cuz. We cool.

DEN

They can fly in ghetto-birds, bro.

CASE

Them nasty fuckin' birds shit light-beams
all over yo ass after midnight.

DEN

It's great to paint with you again, Case.
Made my whole summer, dog.

CASE

Hell yeah, now shut-up and burn, bruh.
Ain't a bingo-party.

A *ghetto-bird* is a police helicopter, a
graffiti artist's worse nightmare; those and
police dogs.

Den and Case have run from both and been
caught by a both. They started painting
together when Den was only nine and could
barely hold a spray-can, he was always
bitching about that, it really bothered him.

Case and Den's brother were twelve already,
they could handle a spray-can fine, they were
kings to him. There wasn't anything in the
whole city those two couldn't climb and
heroically deface with their monikers. Den's
brother's *tag-name* was Kyre; his birth name
spelled backwards.

Every graffiti artist has a tag-name, which
is a *pen-name* they use to not only describe

their *alter-ego* but also disguise their true
identity.

ALLEY - LATER

   Blast drops to the dumpster like a boulder
on a gong in a *Buddhist Temple*, a massive
clashing of metal follows. Case lands with
ninja-skills and they run across the street
into the shadows of a closed store-front.

   Blast was already best friends with Den when
he started tagging with his older brother, so
Blast decided to go out with them. He always
wanted to be a comic-book artist, never
pictured himself tagging that's for sure.
Blast pictured himself in well air-conditioned
office at *Marvel Comics* drawing panels for hit
series *Luchete*.

   Luchete is a Mexican superhero he created
that was overweight and killed people with
food items like tortillas or chilies, he was
sure it would be a hit.

   That changed after Blast experienced the
first rush of raw, potent, unbridled energy
coursing through every cholesterol filled vein
in his body when he caught the *birth tag* of
his new persona with a *Cyclone Super-fat* on a
high-pressure 600 ml *Ironlak Reload*.

   Blast's new future would be written in
aerosol at midnight on a *mailbox* off Ocean
Boulevard; there was no turning back after his
trigger-finger activated that *fat-cap* igniting
a blast of aerosol madness a foot wide.

STORE-FRONT - SAME TIME

   Case and Blast slyly peer out from the
safety of the inset doorway, fuzzy rain
misting around their faces, they stare toward

that mighty canvas in the sky where a shadow rises in front of the billboard, silhouetted as if some morbid defender of the poor, an urban vigilante seeking justice on the streets, justice for his boredom, justice for his poverty, justice for his over-worked mother, justice for his murdered brother, and perhaps a little justice for whatever the fuck suits him best for once.

Den bends over, removing the cloth from the blinding billboard lights, pouring shocking white rays that fill the burgundy sky, igniting those new bent and twisted letters painted over the Coke ad.

They painted the name of their *secret crew* in the same cursive style as the previous *ribboned* and interconnected letters, all filled in with that fiery cola-rouge.

The billboard now reads: *Drink UnKnown-Artists*

BLAST

Those letters are so nasty, Case.

CASE

Got ill styles, B.

Den's outline moves briskly down from the billboard like a cut out from a graphic novel. They watch his black-aura glide across the rooftop, down the fire-ladder, out of the alley and across the street in mere moments.

Den joins them, admiring their work, disposing of his surgical gloves. Case snaps some pics on his cell-phone—

DEN

Careful getting' your ass to Santa Monica, Case.

CASE

Always, cuz, you know me.

DEN

See you in school, Blast.

BLAST

Later kooks!

They break out in different directions, leaving the oil glossed streets behind, leaving their art behind as if worthless. Hanging from the heavens, a new edition to the street museum, *Un-Known Artists* make their mark, leaving a piece of themselves behind.

Floating above Venice, California, vandals rebrand a multi-national corporate advertisement to suit their artistic ends; catching-fame.

I know graffiti is a touchy subject, we all do, that doesn't make it illegitimate as an art form. Sure, it's done on places people don't want and without permission, yet who gave permission to be bombarded with grandiose mass marketing campaigns, who gave permission to be treated like industrial lab-rats in a sprawling shopping mall, forced to buy shit we don't need or want but will never use?

It's like being thrown in a blender filled with useless receipts and old price-tags or drowning inside one of those stupid claw machines at *Denny's* you will never in a million-five years ever get anything back out of no matter how many dollar bills you shove down its' throat.

DEN'S BEDROOM - NIGHT

Den's claustrophobic bedroom is cluttered with teen shit, band posters, many drawings, clothes everywhere, overcrowded art desk, several skateboards, a surfboard, two single beds across from each other, one un-made and well slept in, the other freshly made as if never used. Along another wall are stacks of milk-crates filled with all different spray-paint, expertly color coordinated.

Cans of *Ironlak, Spanish Montana, German Montana, Evolve, Molotow, MTN Hardcore, All-City, Kobra* high and low-pressure, *Plutonium*, even *Rustolium, Krylon*, and *Painters Touch*, too many to name here. Jars of tips in an array of shapes and colors sit on top of the crates. White *Astro-fats*, blue *Cyclone-caps*, *NY fats* and *thins*, yellow *German Universals*, clear *Ghetto Blasters*, black *German-skinnies*, green *Sharp-shooters*, hundreds of them.

One wall has been spray-painted with a mural of a wild jungle scene, many flowering plants, a huge python wearing sun-glasses, a gorilla on the turn-tables, and a toucan with a microphone. His characters have larger heads then bodies, distorted features, stretched limbs, big hands and feet, and though very cartoon-like, the shading makes them look realistic, lighting techniques mind-blowing, alive on the wall.

Den sneaks in the window, sliding his backpack under his bed. The light comes on, startling him—

CONNIE

Let me see your hands. Now.

His mother, Connie, thirty-six years young with a hard life creasing her beautiful face, stands at the door.

                         DEN

            I was over at Fyre's, mom.

She storms over, grabbing his hands, checking them. Nothing is on them, no dirt, no paint, perfectly clean. Connie sighs, relieved but untrusting.

She looks at him sternly—

                        CONNIE

        You can't keep sneaking out, Den. You're
                       sixteen—

                         DEN

                 Don't start in—

                        CONNIE

        Sixteen, Den! Not eighteen. Not yet. I
        know what you get into out there, I won't
        have it, understand?! Life is hard enough
                without this crap.

Den breaths deep, not wanting to hear it, Connie is persistent; concerned.

                         DEN

            I got school in four hours.

                        CONNIE

        I thought you broke up with Fyre?

Den *shrugs*, shutting her out, pushing her far away to keep her safe from the truth. Connie lost one son in a fit of violence on the unforgiving streets; Den is her baby, so he lies to keep her from worrying about him.

Frustrated but powerless over Den, she starts to go, stopping at the door—

                    CONNIE

        Your brother snuck out, all the time, and
                 look where he is.

                     DEN

          I'm not my brother... I'm me.

Connie shakes her head, exasperated, closing the door sternly. Sometimes the sound of a *hard-closed* door is all that need be heard to get your point across.

Den stands there a moment lost in thought, surveying his miniscule kingdom, eyes falling on the well-kept bed. He breaths deep; no-one said life was going to be easy but no said it would be this tough. Den goes to his drawing table, turning on the light.

Piles of sketches, drawing books, markers, pens, pencils, an airbrush, everything needed to bring his imaginings to life. He checks a drawing on his desk, a wild-style 3-D piece with a female Asian anime character spinning records, the lettering reads: FYRE TUF

Fyre is the first love of his life, TUF stands for *"The Unstoppable Force"*, the graffiti crew she and Den are in together. As far as Den knows Fyre is unaware of his involvement in *UnKnown Artists*, after all he and Case are banned by the streets from hanging-out together, but more on that later.

Den crumbles the drawing, clenched fist pulsing, tossing his old flame into an overflowing trashcan then turns off the light, plunging his bedroom into darkness.

CHAPTER TWO - HARD-KNOCK LIFERS

DEN'S APARTMENT - VENICE BEACH - MORNING

Den and Connie's apartment is a classic
seventies style wooden wreck of a building
sitting just off a main drag on an alley.
Obviously built in the seventies based on the
shit architecture, likely hasn't been painted
since then either. The building is for sale
but I doubt anyone would buy it; really it
should be torn down.

An upstairs door opens revealing Den,
backpack on and skateboard in hand. He hustles
downstairs putting his headphones on, dropping
his skateboard he pushes off down the street.

STREETS OF VENICE - DAY

Music blaring in his ears, Den skates
maniacally, busting *mad-tricks* along deserted
morning sidewalks; rocks a tail-slide on a
parking-curb, busts an ollie-flip over a lost
poodle, Jesus-flip over some dog shit,
hospital-flips off a curb on a red light
causing car horns to honk in panic and anger.

Den pretty much turns the urban jungle
around him into a personal playground, dis-
regarding any city-dweller in his path. He
tails-slides past a freshly painted gunmetal-
grey dumpster, leaving his board Den takes a
hot-pink Meanstreak from his pocket and tags
'Den TUF' Crew. Then takes out a black *Krink
Marker*, crosses himself out, tagging *UKA* next
to it, laughing to himself as he hops back on
his skate-board, pushing off.

Den skates up to the corner where the billboard lives from last night. Three teens stare at it, one takes a picture. Den smiles to himself, feeling accomplished he *tic-tacs* down the street, running late.

The advertisement on the new billboard now reads, "Drink *UnKnown Artists"* in that classic Coke font.

VENICE HIGH SCHOOL - MORNING

Venice High School, where the movie *"Grease"* was filmed and where so many far less well known events happen on the daily, has been on Venice Boulevard for near ninety years.

The school's current *art-deco facade* hasn't changed since it was re-built in the 1930's after an earthquake damaged beyond repair the previous *Romanesque styled* building erected a decade earlier. The twenty-nine acre campus is a bit run-down; twelve foot high fences surround the school making it look more like a penitentiary then a place servicing refined public education.

Hundreds of students mill about, getting ready for the day, every race, religion, economic-strata, and trend are represented. Den skates to the front of a soft-white concrete building, pops his board into his hand, and enters as the school bell rings out.

ART CLASS - DAY

Inside room 169 an art class is in full swing. The arts program at Venice High is very good, plenty of quality materials to work with and passionate students who work diligently on their projects. The art teacher, an attractive Afro-American woman in her fifties, dressed casually, hair natural, attitude immensely positive, walks the class, checking on her student's progress while addressing them.

Dolores Roberta Morrison, named after her late grandmother, grew up in Venice and went through it all. One thing she has always been is an incredible artist, which ended up saving her life.

Her family was involved with Boardwalk Hustler Crips or BHC, a gang that started in the seventies as Boardwalk Hustlers then mutated into a Crip set in the eighties. Her father and Uncle started Boardwalk Hustlers in 1970 in order to consolidate their heroin and speed business, which they did very well until crack hit in the eighties; that shit ruined everything.

Delores was in her late teens when her brother became a Hustler, so she became a Hustler too. They mainly sold drugs, some were into pimping prostitutes, others armed robbery, plenty of petty theft. Delores hustled for her art mostly, eventually making a splash in the local art scene, gravitating away from a life of crime. That's when she decided to get her teaching credentials and eventually found herself at the same school she graduated from.

MRS. MORRISON

Art is not about fame or fortune, it can't be. It has to come from some place real. Those of you who have that in you, that burning need for expression, this is where you will find your therapy. Art will save your life one day. When you are troubled, paint. Angry, sculpt. Sad, sketch. Happy, confused, scared, all of it goes into your art.

MRS. MORRISON

You have to be well-rounded, not cornered
by one medium, you must not be afraid to
explore the world of art.

Den works on a clay sculpture of an
abstractly shaped woman, angular and sleek,
amazing for being just sixteen.

MRS. MORRISON

That's what I'm talking about, Dennis. I
love that impressionistic approach,
abstract yet realistic.

Den smiles, pleased to be appreciated.

MRS. MORRISON

You sign up for the scholarship
competition USC is sponsoring? Chance of
a lifetime, Den.

DEN

You're funny, Mrs. Morrison.

Den continues his work, sculpting
meticulously.

MRS. MORRISON

Because I believe in you? I think you can
win, get a scholarship, change your life.

DEN

Not even thinking about that. Be lucky to
graduate High School.

Mrs. Morrison suddenly gets very serious—

22

MRS. MORRISON

You have a gift, a real gift, talent
beyond words; quit pissing it away on the
streets—

Den instinctively cuts her off, feeling
attacked.

DEN

Graffiti isn't piss, it's the new
renaissance. It's the voice of my
generation, that's how we talk.

MRS. MORRISON

That's how you talk, look at her, him,
and them—

Den looks around the room, everyone is
working on different projects, all good for
what they are.

MRS. MORRISON

Out of forty-three students, you are the
only graffiti artist, Dennis.

DEN

That's what's up, Mrs. M, I'm an
original. I paint on concrete.

MRS. MORRISON

Being different is your strong point,
don't lose that, but also, don't lose
yourself to the illusion of the streets.
I know what I'm talking about; I'm O-G
Venice. Just think about it.

Den nods his head in bored agreement as Mrs.
Morrison walks away. He stares at his
sculpture, mind racing, life swirling around

him like the great tornado twisting around Dorothy's house in *The Wizard of Oz*. Den grips the table, sweat bubbling above his lip and forehead; reaching for his sculpture he squeezes its head, squashing soft clay through the creases of his aggravated fingers.

VENICE HIGH - DAY

The quad is filled with students, the sound of *teenage-chatter* is deafening, and how perilously close it all seems to absolute chaos is nerve-racking.

Den emerges from a building, crossing through the throngs to a far corner where graffiti writers from different crews hang out, Blast and TUF Crew included. Den and Blast slyly smile at one-another, having a secret is dangerous but a whole lot of fun.

The general mood of the Venice High student body is certainly up-beat with an underlying palpability of violence and the unknown. Den glances at a group of dangerous looking teenage *cholos* from the oldest known Hispanic gang in Venice.

CYCLONES 13, or C-13 as they initial it, are the most powerful Latino gang in Venice. The gang started in the 1950's with a group of *Zuit-suiters* who grew up in Venice and called themselves *"The Cyclones"*, adopting the number "13" as a numerical code for the letter "M", representing the word *Mota*, or *marijuana*, which they actively sold and proudly smoked. Spray-painting C-13 on a wall was a cheap way to advertise where you could purchase weed.

About *thirty* teenage Cyclones 13 gang members hang out along a low wall at the back of the quad, dressed in baggy *Dickies*, *Nike*

24

Cortez shoes, pressed white t-shirts, black and white bandanas draped from pockets and necks, surely some too old to still be in high-school by the hair on their faces.

Fifteen *cholas*, damn sexy with black lip-stick, painted on eyebrows, teased bangs filled with *Aqua-Net*, hang with them.

One of the Cyclones is a rough, pock-faced white-boy with jet-black hair, vulture-like posture, crooked teeth; his homies call him *Casper*. He stands with his primero homeboy *Sueno*, a Mexican youth with chiseled features and enough *Tres-Flores* in his hair to grease a locomotive. If he wasn't selling drugs or trying to kill people he could be a model. Casper and Sueno step away from the group to mad-dog Den as he passes. For those *not* in the know, *mad-dogging* is when you threaten with eyes, not fists.

Den looks away, wanting nothing to do with their bullshit, nearly bumping into Ra-One from TUF Crew, a tough, scrappy Hispanic teen dressed like a *rapper*, if that makes sense.

RA-ONE

See that UKA billboard on Lincoln? Lame ass *Coca-Cola* font, fuckin toy-ass bitches. I'm-a cross that shit out with my own feces, homie. Fuck UKA.

DEN

Toys crossed me out on Lincoln.

Den and Ra join the rest of TUF Crew, which is only three other teens. Ra-One is the self-proclaimed leader; Syne is sixteen, Afro-American, super lanky, lazy eyes from too much weed, blindly follows Ra's lead. Fyre is a

smoking-hot Afro-Asian, so hot it's tough for
Den to look at her, dressed like a *post-
apocalyptic anime-babe;* hormonal-teen-torture,
especially since she and Den used to date.

SYNE

Who is UKA anyway?

Den sits away from Fyre, trying to act cool,
trying to keep his bruised ego from showing.
Fyre doesn't look at him anyway, just sketches
in her black-book.

DEN

Heard they were from San Francisco.

RA-ONE

Better quit bombing Venice.

FYRE

Ra crossed out C-13 and put UKA on the
boardwalk yesterday.

Den and Blast share a knowing glance, not
good news. Fyre takes a curt gander at Den, he
can't tell if she knows his secret or not.

When Den and Case decided to start a *fake*
graffiti crew over the summer so they could go
bombing together, they never knew what a
hornets nest it would stir up.

Case and Den can't be seen or known to hang
out together because Case, like Den's older
brother, are both from a Santa Monica gang
called *Ghost Town Crips*, or GTC, or GT's for
Ghost Towners. They're a predominantly black
gang that started around Woodlawn Cemetery
near Santa Monica Jr. College in 1980 and have
had beef with Cyclones 13 for thirty years.

Any relations Den is seen to still have with Ghost Town Crips since his brother died could spell certain death for him too. It is a well-known rumor that C-13 was behind the trigger of his brother's murder but no-one was caught, and cops didn't seem to give a fuck.

DEN

Why would you do that, Ra?

RA-ONE

Toys, bro, they bomb Venice, they ain't from Venice, fuck 'em. Hate them fools.

FYRE

We got that battle this weekend, you guys gonna come hard, right? We gotta be on our *A-game*.

Battle is the cultural slang used to describe graffiti crews competing to see who is better by painting dueling murals in aerosols on whatever surface they agree upon.

BLAST

Yeah, my bro's having a party later. Wanna DJ, Fyre? We're charging five at the door, I can pay a little. Have to bring your equipment though.

FYRE

Hell yes I wanna DJ. Have your brother pick me up in his truck so I can bring everything.

Blast puts his hand out like he wants a *five*, she scratches his palm like a DJ, using her other hand as a headphone, making scratching noises with her mouth.

                    RA-ONE

    We're battling TBS Crew from the valley.
    Gotta come clean with them characters,
    Den, The Bomb Society are mad-dope,
        especially this fool YaYa.

                     DEN

          I'm sick of characters.

                    RA-ONE

    Too bad, that's what you do best. Me and
    Syne do letters, you do characters, Fyre
    and Blast do background. That's how we
    win; TUF is now The Unstoppable *Five*,
                 fuck force.

    Den looks away, peeved, but trying not to
    show it, for him it is just another day at
    Venice High.

VENICE GRAFFITI WALLS - LATE DAY

    Sun blazes like a great gas-lantern, heating
    the day to scorching temperatures as
    skateboarders bust lip-slides and suski-
    grinds, ollie-to-fackies, stalefish-grabs,
    stiffies, tuck-knees, judo-airs, nose-grabs
    (and any other weird two-words you can slap
    together) at the gnarly beach-front *Venice
    Skate Park*.

    The boardwalk is a mad-assortment of the
    unusual and bizarre, tattooed and dangerous,
    drugged out and homeless, all tossed together
    with a plethora of sunburned tourists; a
    strange, eclectic mash; a living circus.

    Venice has everything to offer all walks of
    life, a paradise for homeless as well as
    housed. Want a great meal? Go to Venice. Need
    a tan? Go to Venice. Looking to get drunk? Go

to Venice. Want to paint a wall? Venice is your spot.

The famed remains of the once abandoned Venice Beach Amphitheater, also built by Abbot Kinney, where writers from all over L.A. came to catch a tag or do a piece back in the eighties. Thanks to the hard work of a few old-school writers from Venice, *graffiti-artists* from all over the world still paint it to this very day. Unfortunately all that's left standing are two rather long six-foot high walls and several tipi shaped concrete bbq smoke-stacks set aside for graffiti artists to paint on weekends.

The walls get so many layers of paint on them that at the going rate by the year 2050 there will be an added 30 feet of thickness to the wall or something like that, I don't remember exactly. They get painted a whole fucking lot is what I mean. If you paint in the morning, it will be gone by afternoon; that said, it's best to paint late Sunday afternoon that way it will ride at least until the following Saturday. Notoriously taggers hit them at night all throughout the week, so there's really no hope.

Venice graffiti walls are still a beautiful, iconic place to paint, during the off season the perfect place to chill, smoke a blunt, catch a burner, and waste the day away.

Den and Blast are at the walls painting their names, not trying to come hard, just doing what they love. The lettering on both pieces is clean and simple, like lettering from a comic-book cover. Even though it's not the weekend and they aren't supposed to, they paint anyway. Fuck it right? What else is there to do after school?

Tourists pass in droves; many take pictures
of the graffiti art and the boys painting.
Blast pressed hard on *Pink-dot, Roark-black*
line flaring out like an afro, pulling it hard
to a point sharp as a rat tail, paint spitting
dry, sweat glazing his cheeks *chili-rojo*, he
collapses in a heap, taking a Gatorade from
his backpack, drinking deep.

<u>BLAST</u>

Wish Case could be there Saturday, I love
painting with him, if we had him instead
of Ra we'd be killin' it.

Blast gazes longingly as a group of bikini-
clad girls pass.

<u>DEN</u>

If he wasn't in Ghost Town he could.
Cyclones hate them.

<u>BLAST</u>

So stupid, man. Can't believe Ra. That
dumb-ass crossed out C-13 and wrote UKA,
we're dead if they find out. Especially
you, homeboy, they already hate you.

<u>DEN</u>

My brother was in Ghost Town, not me.
They'll never know who we are.

Den slips his headphones on, closing himself
off from this cold, dark world. Troubled since
his dad left when he was only six, Den's new
father-figure quickly became his older
brother. He stuck to him like a shadow; trying
to be like him, act like him, dress like him.

Den's older brother introduced him to
tagging and bombing, his brother got him

stoned the first time, drunk the first time, even got him laid the first time.

But *gang-life* changed all that, in very short-order Den found himself torn between two worlds; one being the violent, twisted world of his brother, one being his own riotous aerosol-fueled urban-rebellion; unleashing a savage artistic revolution upon an unwary society, upon lowly buildings and barren walls, upon desolate underpasses, lonely overpasses, wayward bridges and forsaken tunnels, vacant trains and *dismal* sewers, the more hauntingly-abandoned the better.

A beautiful blonde haired perfectly polished diamond glides up as if floating on Aether, not dressed for the beach, but a welcome site for any eyes. Maple is sixteen and in from Bel Air on a *photo-safari* for a school project.

Blast sees Maple; perking up he wipes sand-riddled sweat from his face, trying to sort himself should they have an encounter. She takes photos nearby with a brand new camera, brand new camera bag, and brand new smile.

Maple catches Blast looking at her, which draws her attention to Den, immediately she feels something stir inside of her, like a serpent coiling. She stops looking for pictures to take and watches him paint. So relaxed and free, so focused and messy, talented and different, tanned and handsome.

Uncontrollably drawn forward she walks toward Den, acting casual while checking out his work. Blast can't believe she's so close to them, his spastic-hormones kicking like an unbroken horse.

Den is oblivious, headphones and cheap sun-glasses on, painting to an unheard *track*.

MAPLE

That's really good.

Den doesn't hear her, head filled with *trap-music*, focus riveted on his work. Blast tosses his Gatorade cap at Den, hitting the wall in front of him. He pulls his headphones down, Blast nods for Den to look behind him.

Den turns, instantly dumbfounded by Maple's beauty, can of paint slipping from his hand, landing at his feet in the burning sand. Maple smirks but maintains composure, raised to never sweat under pressure, brought up courageously independent.

MAPLE

That's really good.

DEN

Nah, it's a'right though.

Den half smiles, grabbing the spray-can from the sand; he tries to paint nonchalantly as Blast chuckles. Not often has Blast seen Den flustered, this is an entertaining first.

MAPLE

You mind if I take some pictures?

DEN

You a cop? Look like one.

Den half-smiles at her, Maple half-smiles back.

MAPLE

Yeah, totally am...

BLAST

If you're a cop then arrest me 'cause I'm guilty of everything and definitely need to be punished.

Den shakes his head then shrugs at Maple—

DEN

Sure, take some flicks…

BLAST

Not of me though, I mean you're hot as fish-grease but I don't want my picture taken, cool?

MAPLE

As an igloo.

She takes a picture of Den painting with a *Super-skinny* on a low-pressure *Mango Hardcore*. He screws up a key line, cracking under the pressure of her presence, a billion neurons shooting like fireworks through his brain.

Maple sees his nervousness, feels it, everyone feels it when it happens, there's no hiding it when raw attraction meets youthful vivacity, awkward tension always obvious yet we hide it; play it cool. I wonder how many beautiful relationships never saw the light of day because we were playing it *too cool*?

MAPLE

What does it say?

DEN

Says you're beautiful.

Maple's natural smile shines from so deep it
would take an excavator and drilling machine
to uncover its origins.

                    MAPLE

        Yuh, right. D-E-N? Just Den?

                     DEN

        Short for Dennis. What's yours?

She snaps a close up of him as he takes off
his sunglasses.

                    MAPLE

          Maple, like the syrup.

   She snaps one more photo of him staring into
her lens with piercing green eyes, his mural
behind him.

                     DEN

         Photography, huh? Can I see?

   She hands him the camera but instead of
looking at the pictures, he aims it at her,
she sticks out her tongue as he snaps a photo,
then takes a picture of Blast—

                    BLAST

       Sheeez, now the pigs got my picture.

Den hands her back the camera.

                    MAPLE

        I'll delete them if you want. Or I can
        send you copies. What's your e-mail? Or I
        can DM them to you on IG, whatever. You
                  have Flicker?

                        DEN

               Don't have that.

                       MAPLE

             Email or Instagram?

                        DEN

                     Neither.

                       MAPLE

               Twitter? Facebook?

Den sheepishly shrugs in the negative.

                       MAPLE

                  You're kidding?

                        DEN

             Don't have a computer.

                       MAPLE

           You don't have a computer?

                        DEN

      A lot of people don't. In fact, most of
             the world is computer free.

                       MAPLE

                What's your cell?

                        DEN

               Sorry. Cell-less.

                       MAPLE

                      Pager?

                        DEN

        Come on? Now that's funny. Call my home.

He grabs a can of *Love-pink*, tagging his
number on a piece of soda stained card-board
lying in the sand, awkwardly giving it to her.

It's large and she has nowhere to put it. She
looks at him in a way that betrays her,
instantly transported to the imaginary-
metaphysical-dreamscape; Den illuminating her.

MAPLE

Alright. Hmm… Nice to meet you.

She slowly walks away, feeling his presence
drifting she can't help but glance over her
shoulder at him.

BLAST

Now that bitch is fine.

DEN

Way out of my league. Way out.

They can't help but watch her walk away,
heat of the sun ice-cold compared to Maple.
She's fuckin' hot.

CHAPTER THREE — LIFE OF THE QUEEN
STREETS OF BEL AIR, CALIFORNIA — DAY

Bel Air is a lush and beautiful community for the exceedingly wealthy resting at the foothills of the Santa Monica Mountains, it's part of LA's *Platinum Triangle* along with Holmby Hills and Beverly Hills. Next to Malibu, the most expensive real-estate you can find in Los Angeles.

A farmer named Alphonzo Bell from Santa Fe Springs, California struck it rich when oil was discovered on his land. Just like *The Beverly Hill Billies* his farming-family moved to Los Angeles, buying a large ranch far outside of down-town. He sectioned the land off, built roads, landscaped it and in 1923 called it *Bel Air, California*.

Alphonzo then founded the relaxing Bel Air Beach Club in Santa Monica and luxurious Bel Air Country Club off Sunset Boulevard above UCLA, drawing the wealthy-elite to his properties like flies to shit. Very rich flies that is; to some very expensive shit that is.

Maple drives through the hills of Bel Air in her brand new BMW SUV listening to hip-hop and rapping along, not a care in the world.

Passing outside her limo-tint windows are luxurious mansions with ample greenery sprawling in all directions.

She pulls up to a massive iron gate blocking entry to an elusive estate beyond, rolls down her window, places her thumb on a scanner; one beep later, the gate opens.

Maple's Beamer rides up a windy, well-groomed drive, passing several gardeners who trim away at plush foliage.

She parks in front of an extravagant Mediterranean-style mansion beside a Tesla and Range Rover; it's like a high-end car-lot.

Happy and free, she hops out of her SUV, grabbing the large cardboard business card, skip-walking toward the family home; still rapping acapella like a pro.

BEL AIR MANSION - DAY
The mansion is immaculately decorated as if pulled from the pages of *Architectural Digest*, grand maple staircase with etched railings wrapping widely around a marble floored entry. Maple enters through oversize double-doors, extra light in the feet she glides through the foyer calling out for her father. She stops in the middle of a classy lounge room, outfitted with a proper bar, several hundred inch flat-screens hanging from the walls.

The lounge is decorated in rich mahogany wood panels, Tuscan columns, fully stocked bar appointed with saddle-leather bar-stools, couches, and chairs, all surrounded in a lush tropical motif.

Maple takes out her *iPhone* and tries her dad's cell—

MAPLE

Where are you? —Oh, I see you.

She looks out the window, a fit, handsome six-foot-five giant stands by the pool, waving; she waves back.

BEL AIR MANSION POOL - MOMENTS LATER

Maple walks from the house toward the large, rectangular blue-bottom pool where her father, George G. Baker III, late forties insanely successful corporate law attorney, tans to a golden brown.

George was born rich, raised rich, became even richer, and still earns twenty million per year; which in Bel Air is a pittance, but with an inheritance of three-hundred million dollars that his father made as a real-estate mogul, the old Beverly Hills hacienda was upgraded to a Bel Air estate very quickly. George's attitude has always been work hard, live hard, party hard, but do it healthy, and never get addicted to anything but success.

Rosita, their Cuban maid, early sixties Hispanic with long wrinkles across her expressionless face, delivers a Mojito, to George as Maple arrives at the pool from the main house. George drinks deep, spotting the cardboard with a spray-painted number on it.

GEORGE BAKER

What the hell is that?

Maple looks down at Den's number—

MAPLE

Just a number, I took some photos of an
artist in Venice—

GEORGE BAKER

What have I told you about that? You are
not to go down there, young lady. Hear
me?

MAPLE

It's my school project, dad. It's Venice
or skid-row in DTLA. You worked near
skid-row didn't you? Want me wandering
around down there in my school uniform
snapping pictures of bums?

GEORGE BAKER

You want pictures of bums then take a
photo of our gardeners in the front yard
when they aren't looking, no one will
know the difference.

George polishes off the Mojito in a gulp.

GEORGE BAKER

Boy, Rosita makes a good Mojito.

He stands, stretching, walking to the crystal-
blue pool.

GEORGE BAKER

I'm going to Vegas for the weekend;
you'll be in the office alone Saturday.
Throw that number out. I don't want you
calling some Venice Beach freak.

MAPLE

I'm not calling him.

                    GEORGE BAKER

        You're not allowed there. You want the
          beach; go to Malibu, plenty of bums
        there, I know, I represent them in court.
                 Corporate bums.

                      MAPLE

              Why no Venice, dad?

He looks at her sternly—

                    GEORGE BAKER

         You know why. You need something?

                      MAPLE

                  Forget it.

She turns and walks away, that once bright
glow now dimmed and dull. He turns and dives
in the pool.

MAPLE'S BEDROOM - LATER

Maple's bedroom is perfectly decorated in a
Caribbean theme, expensive tropical paintings,
matching bed-set and dressers, walk-in cedar-
lined closet, massive bay window looking out
over the Santa Monica Mountains, a truly
magical place to be young, or old, or dead.

Rosita exits Maple's bathroom with some
dirty towels—

                      ROSITA

        Laundry, laundry, too much laundry.

Rosita's family moved from Miami to Los
Angeles in the late sixties, but came to
America from Cuba during the Cuban Missile
Crisis in the early sixties; father convinced

it was WWIII and Havana was to be flatted into an atomic wasteland like Hiroshima.

Her father sold everything they had, which wasn't much, and bought their way into Florida, settling in Miami. Her parents dreamed of opening a Cuban restaurant but found the competition far too great in Miami.

Once again, Rosita's father sold everything they owned, which wasn't much, moving them two-thousand-seven-hundred and thirty miles across a foreign land to Los Angeles where after years of struggle they opened what would become a very successful café called *La Leche de Cuba* in down-town Los Angeles.

Rosita worked at *La Leche de Cuba* her whole life, hating every minute due to her father treating his family like slaves, forcing them to do all the work at the café and *la casa de familia*, rarely paying them.

Fortunately for Rosita the café was frequented by George III when he was a young partner at a corporate law firm in down-town. After complaining to him one too many times about the terrible situation with her family, George did what any sensible rich Californian would do; he hired her as his maid.

Maple sits at her immaculate desk about to upload the pictures to her computer, looking instead *at* the computer, bemused.

MAPLE

No computer?

ROSITA

You say something, mija?

She smiles, plugging in her memory card—

MAPLE

Nothing, Rosita, just talking to myself.

Rosita continues on out with the towels in her arms.

ROSITA

Oh I do this all the time!

Maple turns on some music as she uploads her many photos. They start popping up on her screen; most are of locations and objects, all very well framed, but many are of homeless women, their faces drawn and sad, with hopeless gazes and vacant eyes.

She takes a photo of a beautiful woman in her thirties from her desk, comparing it to the homeless women, the fullness of life and vibrant smile in the picture is incomparable to those hardened, haunted, lifeless persons in her photographs from Venice. She touches the woman's face, closing her eyes so she can feel her presence; it's been so long since she saw her, so very, very long.

An E-Vite pops up on her computer screen:

"DON'T FORGET JESSICA'S SWEET SIXTEEN THIS SATURDAY NIGHT! BE THERE OR BE NOBODY!"

Maple places the picture of her mother back in the drawer then returns to scrolling her photos until she finds the ones of Den, emerald-green eyes smiling at her and the one of him in sunglasses. She zooms into the sunglasses, a perfect image of herself reflected in them.

There is something about this kid Den; she can't quite figure it out but is convinced there is a deeper meaning to their introduction; a sublime significance has planted itself deep inside her mind like the seed to a mustard tree, a great wonder may grow from it.

Maple looks at the large piece of cardboard—

DEN'S APARTMENT - SAME TIME

Connie's phone rings as Den finishes stacking a multi-layer PBJ sandwich in their tiny kitchen. The sink is overflowing with dishes and counters covered in old containers, wrappers, plates, coffee cups, whatever.

Den hurries to the phone and answers—

DEN

Hello. (he listens for a moment) Like the syrup, yeah-- (he smiles wide) Sure, meet me in Venice tomorrow, we're battling a crew from the valley, maybe you can photograph the slaughter for us.

MAPLE'S BEDROOM - SAME TIME

Maple plays with the photo of Den on her editing software, enhancing colors, bringing out hidden hues in the sky, increasing saturation of colors in his painting.

MAPLE

I can't, I have to work... (Listens, smiling) My dad's office in Beverly Hills, it sucks. Can I call later?

DEN'S APARTMENT - SAME TIME

Den sits on a worn couch, biting into his six-slice PB&J sandwich, jelly drips on his shirt, pants, floor, everywhere.

                    DEN

        Just call me, whenever. You know?

MAPLE'S BEDROOM - SAME TIME

   Maple zooms in to Den's eyes enhancing the
shades of green. She hits print on the tool
bar—

                   MAPLE

         Sure. Do you want my number?

DEN'S APARTMENT - SAME TIME

   Den wipes jelly off his shirt while trying
to get comfortable on the small, threadbare
couch; its thin cushions give way to easy.

                    DEN

      Nah, that's just not realistic to me.
           I'll wait to hear from you.

He hangs up, staring at the phone curiously.
Impossible. Never in his life did he imagine
Maple would actually call him. He grabs a pen
and starts tagging her name "Maple" over and
over again on a small pad of paper. Finally
catching himself, Den stops, tears the sheet
from the pad and crumbles it up.

   Den examines a picture of himself at eight
with his mom and brother cuddled up at the
beach, wishing he was little again, wishing he
could not care again.

MAPLE'S BEDROOM - SAME TIME

   Maple stares at her phone, curiously. Did he
just hang up? The photo of Den drops out of
the printer. Maple picks it up, holding it

                                              45

carefully. Den smiles sheepishly in the picture, his face showing a deeper life experience, a quiet sadness in his eyes, a creative spirit so vivid it shines. Maple smiles as if Den is in the room with her.

Her dad pokes his head in, wet from the pool—

GEORGE BAKER

You throw that number away?

She hides the picture, picking the tagged cardboard from her desk, cramming it in a small trashcan. The cardboard is too big but after a few strategic folds and forceful cramming, she gets it in.

MAPLE

Happy?

GEORGE BAKER

I want you to be careful who you get involved with, that's all. That fella Grant, I like him. Great family, plays lacrosse, good taste in bourbon too.

She rolls her eyes, shaking her head.

MAPLE

Dad, please let me off Saturday, please? Jessica wants a girl's day before the party. It's her sweet-sixteen, please?

She gives him the ultimate *'you can't say no to me'* look. George caves in, he is hard on his daughter because he doesn't want her to be weak and make poor life choices like her mother did.

George studies her soft features, heart warming up, remembering how adorable and innocent she was as a baby, wanting the world for her, the universe for her.

GEORGE BAKER

You work next Saturday *and* Sunday, deal?

She sighs heavily, miserably agreeing. Her dad is a good dad, even if he hasn't been around much, she knows he loves her and wants her happy, but she doesn't feel whole.

Maple hasn't felt whole since her mother left when she was twelve.

MAPLE

We would know if she was dead, right?

GEORGE BAKER

What you need to know is she made a conscious choice to do what she did, no one forced her, no one pushed her away. I sure as hell didn't.

MAPLE

Forget it. Forget I said anything.

George has nothing more to say, this is a sore subject.

GEORGE BAKER

I will forget, and so should you.

George nods to her; eyes darken with the seriousness of his emotions, closing the door.

Maple looks at her photo of Den, opens the drawer and places it next to the pretty woman in her thirties, the woman who gave birth to her, who became a drunk, then drug addict, then homeless. The woman she calls mother.

CHAPTER FOUR — SECRETS ARE FOREVER
DEN'S BEDROOM — NIGHT

Den is in his *storage-closet* of a bedroom getting some spray-cans together. His mom opens the door letting in Case and Blast.

She notes what he is up to, giving him 'the look'—

<u>DEN</u>

We're just piecing the Venice wall alright? Gonna burn it before the battle tomorrow.

<u>CONNIE</u>

No illegal graffiti. None. I can't deal. I have to work tonight, can you please be home before me?

Den shrugs 'I *guess* so'. She kisses him on the head, tussles his salty locks, and leaves. Blast watches her wantonly; he's had a crush on her since he was ten, and she is still *so hot*. Connie betrays her age with a youthful vibrancy, a connection to life that most lose when they get their first real job. But she hasn't lost it, Blast sees it.

<u>BLAST</u>

Your mom is hot, bro.

<u>DEN</u>

Zip your pie-flaps, sucker. Check out this new style...

Den shows them wicked 3-D futuristic
lettering stretching across a page like some
alien-alphabet spacecraft, each letter a
different section of the ship and says "FIVE
FOR LIFE". It's jaw-dropping.

CASE

That's some next level shit, Den.

BLAST

Ra won't let you do the lettering, he
always has to.

DEN

Yeah, we'll see.

CASE

About tonight—

Case shows them a sketch he did for the
night. It reads, 'UNKNOWN ARTISTS - KINGS OF
VENICE' in warped old English letters with a
blue-chrome fade.

DEN

Bananas, bro. Ra's gonna lose it.

CASE

That's the idea.

VENICE GRAFFITI WALLS - NIGHT

Dark purple hues fill the skyline as a
billion city lights reflect off low, dark
clouds. The outlines of buildings on the
boardwalk sharpen; streetlamps radiate
splitting beams into the night. Den, Case, and
Blast pass a group of homeless sharing a
bottle, crossing a grassy partition, down a
bike path leading toward the graffiti walls.

Once arriving, they immediately get to work, wasting no time, each one with their own task. Case loves painting with high pressure *Kobra paint* with an *Astro-cap*, huge baby *Blue 29* chem-trails spew from the nozzle covering the wall in a single coat. Blast has a *Pink dot* on his blue *Sugar 79* adding a fluffy fade to Case's color. Den outlines a letter, *Rusto-fat* drawing hard on a *Kobra Dark Violet*, he carves a two inch border that needs no *cut-backs*.

Having spent the greater part of ten months bombing together, these three have it down to a science. Barely speaking a word, each handles their part of the mural with precision, Case sketching the letters, Den and Blast filling them in, outlining as they go.

Graffiti is alive, graffiti is a drug, graffiti is addictive, graffiti is a vice; no other art form comes with as much excitement, adventure, risk, or reward then graffiti art. Since mankind was first able to scratch a dick on the walls of Ancient Rome humans have pursued a life of graffiti art. There is a real personal freedom to leaving your mark on everything for everyone to see, a kind of back-alley fame that permeates every part of your being.

Once bitten by that late-night viper, vile toxins fill your veins; aerosol dreams invade your mind, adrenalin flows from a nozzle on a tin can full of your favorite color and must be pressed again and again and again to keep that flow of endorphins and dopamine going on over-time.

Graffiti is an art form that you either embrace for a lifetime, graduate from to other artistic mediums, or leave behind forever in a drunken instant. There's no end to it, all graffiti does is drain you as you continuously refill it with time, energy, and money. Rarely do graffiti writers see a dime from their labors and passion, in fact it is the one artistic medium that *cannot exist in a gallery* or museum, so how can it be sold? Who's supposed to buy it?

Graffiti art cannot be sold, it can only be given away for free on the sides of shot-up liquor stores or down distant train tracks, on the shit-stained walls of dingy alleyways or toxic abandoned factories, anywhere a surface presents itself the graffiti writer finds his canvas. Corrugated metal, brick wall and cinderblock, wood slats and plastic siding, you build it, we paint it.

The real challenge is in the execution, in making the canvas disappear and the image come to life. It is a painful and pointless choice to become a graffiti artist because there is never any permanence out there for your artistic expression; it comes and goes like weather, like frequencies, like relationships.

VENICE BOARDWALK - DAY

Maple approaches the Venice Graffiti Walls with her camera ready, around the walls several tables sit under pop-up tents, a DJ spins music, four camera men and a sound guy ready their equipment as people of all ages gather in anticipation of some exciting event.

All around Maple are skate-boarders, break-dancers, graffiti-artists, street-performers, derelicts, foreigners, and of course, many homeless; she takes photos of them all, exhilarated by this outlandishly creative atmosphere, slowly falling in love with this crazy slice of Americana.

Maple sees a homeless woman in a Dodger's baseball hat lying against a tree, arms sagging from malnutrition, cheek-bones sunk in like a corpse. She studies her, a deep feeling of sadness taking over, filling her entire being with loneliness. She raises her camera, zooms in on the woman and snaps several pictures. Lowering her camera, she sees Den walking up, hair whipping in the morning breeze, eyes ablaze with excitement.

Maple zooms in on him, taking his picture. Den seems to look right at her for a moment, startling her.

For someone who behaves so mature, who regards herself as the smartest girl in the room, she still carries a child-like innocence that is inescapable, especially when it comes to romance.

VENICE GRAFFITI WALLS - DAY

TUF Crew stands in front of the freshly painted mural UKA did just last night and Ra is pissed off.

RA-ONE

I want to know who these bitches are. I am so sick of seeing their faggot-ass tags all over, I dissed a bunch just last night! *Kings of Venice*?! They're from San Francisco!

DEN

Maybe it's TUF Crew's old members? We lost ten heads in six months 'cause they didn't like the way things were run.

RA-ONE

You want to play the king-dick, then you get up on damn near every street between Venice and DTLA. Shit fool, I got more tags in the Valley then most of these toys we're about to battle and they *live* in the fuckin' valley.

DEN

We are hella low on numbers. Five?

RA-ONE

Back in the I-E, TUF Crew is eighty strong, plus mad other chapters all over southern Cali. Losing a few punks that couldn't hang ain't shit.

BLAST

Yeah, but UKA kinda got Venice on lock with all the Heavens and throwies, Ra.

Den and Blast catch a quick look at each other, both loving to chide him without him knowing their undisclosed truth.

RA-ONE

Man, fuck UKA!

ENZONE

I couldn't agree more, Ra.

An old school graff-writer from the 80's steps up; EnzOne, mid-forties, buff as a dock-worker wearing a scraggly beard, cammo-shorts and T-shirt that says "BATTLE ZONE" in dope old-school bubble letters.

EnzOne is their mentor, their *street-guru*, a true graffiti artist that never left the hood behind, always been true to the game. He's been shot twice, stabbed three times, beaten dozens, chased thousands, arrested plenty, and still loves to paint. He runs a graffiti crew battle once a month that streams live on his website *planetstreet.com*.

> ENZONE

These guys are why we got no places to do our art legally. Taggers and illegals, which I respect, but we have to grow beyond that. You know when you rock a fresh wall on my live-stream, more than a million writers world-wide are seeing your work? Talk about getting up.

> SYNE

You were up from San Diego to Sacramento, Enzo. Fuckin' legend, bro. Wasn't for you, none of us would've even started bombing, true-words.

> RA-ONE

I would, I'm All-City-King-Ra-One, fool.

Ra slaps fives with Fyre, young flaring.

> ENZONE

I got fame, it was cool, but I got busted hard, almost ruined my life. Had to do eighteen months in jail, pay a twenty thousand dollar fine; spent eight hundred hours doing community service, it was fucked up shit.

> SYNE

You own a paint company, I'm not crying.

> ENZONE

I worked hard for what I have. Not many people from my generation lived to do much of anything, especially heads from here in Venice. Was it worth it for me?

54

ENZONE

I don't know, I mean I wasn't raised
with shit so was used to not having shit.
After living a gutter life for so long
eventually you have to change, you have
to get with the times, fight for
something other than fame. I still bomb
freights on weekends, I know, I know. I
want your generation to be smarter, think
ahead; don't waste away so long you get
to old to do shit, you don't want to be
an old-fucker that never did nothin'.

RA-ONE

You the only old mutha-fucka round here.

EnzOne has a laugh, honesty breeds humor.

FYRE

Let's just buff this wall and battle.

Ra, Syne, Blast, and Fyre begin buffing the
wall, covering the *UnKown-Artists'* painting
with a goopy coat of *jungle-green* buff paint.

The other graffiti crew walks up; they are
TBS, *"The Bomb Society"*, ten members deep, all
behaving thuggish and crude as they start
buffing the other wall *charcoal-black*.

Their leader, YaYa, an eighteen year old
Pilipino-American, rough around every edge,
big hoops in his ears, well on his way to
being covered in tattoos, looks at Fyre,
sticking his tongue out seductively.

ENZONE

Ignore that shit, TBS are more Tag-
bangers then graffiti artists, what they
lack in humanity, they make up for in
talent. Don't sleep on these dudes.

Tag-bangers are a graffiti crew that behaves
more like a gang; they are far more apt to
violence and prefer to fight than battle. Den
looks at Ya-Ya with a venomous stare as Blasts
pulls on his shirt—

BLAST

Fuck those dudes. Let's just beat 'em on
the wall. Show Ra those new letters.

Den shakes it off, taking his black-book out
of his backpack. He flips it open to his
sketch of the futuristic alien-spacecraft-
letters, showing it to Ra-One who is too busy
buffing to look.

Ra lives off his ego, if it isn't his idea
it's a bad idea. He runs the crew like a
despot and thinks *he* is the freshest bread on
the shelf. Everyone puts up with him because
he is really, really good and he's up from
Venice Beach to Down Town L.A., All-City-King-
Ra-One.

DEN

Ra. Got some new letters. Figure we could
come at TBS with some *space-opera* shit,
you know? I'm sick of characters, bro.

RA-ONE

Homie, you're on characters, that's
final. You rock the dope shit, none of us
got characters like you. Seen TBS's work?

FYRE

They come hard as fuck, especially YaYa.

Yaya, that fool bites Den's whole style.
Long, angular necks, realistic fades,
homie def been studying you, Den. He's
the real thing, homie straight burns.

The slang terms *bite* or *biter* refers to
another artist using your style and claiming
it's original.

Ra opens his sketchbook, the lettering is
all worked out, it reads; UNSTOPPABLE FORCE in
some crazy looking organic letters, like
florescent-green amoebas being ripped apart
and wrapped around each-other. Off to the
sides and in the back-ground of the lettering
are loose sketches of tropical trees with
rudimentary outlines of different jungle
animals. A basic drawing of a toucan holding a
wood sign with the word "THE" carved on it
standing on a branch in front of the rest of
the lettering.

RA-ONE

Just like your bedroom, homeboy. That's
what we're doing.

DEN

Lettering is ill, but we've done a jungle
theme two other times battling here.

RA-ONE

Yeah, bruh, won both times. That's why we
doin' it this time, so we know we win.

SYNE

Like insider trading on these ducks. That
paint sponsorship is ours, doggie.

Den, bummed yet enthusiastic, walks away to
gather himself, seeing Maple approaching TBS'
wall with her camera. She starts taking photos

of Yaya from TBS Crew. Yaya sees her out of
the corner of his eye and stops buffing the
wall, pissed—

YAYA

I got warrants, bitch. Unless you hate
that camera you best stop taking pictures
or it's mine.

Maple is stunned, even shaken by his hostile
energy. She steps back as Den marches over,
shoulders back and chest out, *Peacocking*
without knowing it. His unsettling care for
Maple bleeds from his glands; an unwavering
desire to believe in the possibility of being
with her at constant war with low self-esteem
and a woeful economic status. But nothing
would stop him from defending her, not man nor
beast nor time.

DEN

Then leave the beach, biter.

YaYa starts *mad-dogging* Den, face furrowing
and lip contorting with inner rage. No one
talks-shit to YaYa and gets away with it.

YAYA

What'd you say, fool?

DEN

Biter. What's up Maple?

Maple smiles, relaxing with Den's presence
she changes some settings on her camera.

MAPLE

Not much, just… you know.

YaYa steps so close to Den his baseball hat touches his forehead, Den doesn't flinch.

                    YAYA

    Eh, fucker, we don't have to paint, we
    can just go for a walk down the beach,
                  drop-dogs.

                    DEN

    Sounds romantic. Maybe later when the
            sun's going down.

                    YAYA

    I'll *make* the sun go down, fool.

Fyre and the others watch what's happening, tensions high as TBS Crew gathers around YaYa and Den. Blast, Syne, and Ra man-up, rambling over. Fyre is more interested in checking out Maple; her competition.

Fyre and Den used to be inseparable, they did everything together. After Den's brother died their relationship became deeper, became hopelessly romantic. They were in love but Den was so torn up over his brother's death he became untrustworthy and erratic.

Den's dark times finally led into the Juvenile Justice System, that's where he really learned to fight.

                  ENZONE

            We cool here?

                    YAYA

    No, we ain't. I don't like my picture
                taken, dog.

EnzOne joins them with two of his old-school boys, both biker-tough, far more scary than

YaYa and his crew could ever hope to be.
Everyone settles down—

                    ENZONE

You read the rules on my website? Did you
    agree to them when you or a member of
    your crew signed up? Clause states that
      in order to join *The Battle Zone*, you
    have to let people photograph or film you
                while you paint.

                     YAYA

                     So?

                    ENZONE

Then you didn't read about my deal with
    the Police and the City of Venice to
  organize these opportunities for crews
    from all over to meet and share their
               artistic styles.

    EnzOne points at two sunglass wearing
Bicycle Cops standing twenty yards away—

                     YAYA

            Take your pictures.

    Den and Maple share a relieved smile; Yaya
goes to his wall, pops the top off a spray-
can, shaking it angrily. Den and Maple walk
toward TUF Crew's wall, hands lightly brushing
together, magnetism growing, attraction
obvious as the moon at night.

                    MAPLE

        You always come to the rescue?

                     DEN

      As little as humanly possible, but for
                you? Anytime.

Maple gently bites her lip as she meets eyes
with Fyre for the first time. Fyre cocks her
hip in defiance then turns and goes back to
painting the wall.

DEN

Fyre is my ex-g.

MAPLE

I figured that out at first look.

Blast hands a few cans of grey spray-paint
to Den—

BLAST

We only have five hours, Romeo, let's do
this.

MAPLE

I'll watch for a while, get some photos,
then may walk around a bit, take some
other pictures.

Den doesn't want to look away, not for a
moment. The longer he stares, the harder it is
to imagine not having a chance to know her,
see her often, hold her hand forever.

DEN

Will you be here after?

MAPLE

Maybe I will.

Her Cheshire-grin tells Den *maybe* is *yes*.

DEN

Maybe I'll see you then.

MAPLE

Maybe I'll still be here.

FYRE

Hey Den, lunchtime's over.

DEN

I haven't even had breakfast yet.

Fyre hands a bucket of jungle-green paint to him, causing him to drop his spray-cans, spilling green paint on his shoes. Maple looks at his shoes; they are already covered in all shades of paint, a rubber-soled shit-show.

Maple picks up the spray-cans and hands them back, their hands touching briefly, yet in that moment time ceases to hold influence, not a sound can be heard as a thousand unspoken words are shared between them.

Den gently draws away; she doesn't move an inch, forcing him to part first. Den slips on headphones, going to work buffing the wall.

Maple backs away slowly, taking photos of him, curious about his life story. She finds a place to sit and watches as they create an entire world out of nowhere.

Den and TUF Crew work seamlessly as a team, bringing their *jungle-scene* together with professional ease. Fyre plugs a *Smoky-skinny* on a *Neon-green Molotow*, accenting leaves on a palm-plant, creating an intense light-flare. Blast rocks *Electro-blue* sky fills using *Ironlak* with a *Super-silver fat-cap*, dusting the atmosphere with potent fumes. Ra and Syne build layers of *Ironlak* greens, blending *Chameleon* into *Reals Sublime*, shaded by *Vans Kryptonite* fades adding shape to the splaying, undulating *amoeba-letters*.

Den tirelessly details his characters, dropping a *German-skinny tip* on a low-pressure Montana, fading *Greyhound-brown* with *Toasted-brown*, adding a stencil-tip for magenta lip details on a distorted tree-sloth, dooky gold-chain dangling about its tubular neck.

Den switches to a *NY Fat Cap* on a can of *Ironlak Roark*, his favorite black, to fast fill a black-panther with a *black-fist hair-pick* in his fur, paw raised for *Panther-Power*. He taps a tin of *Miami pink* with a *Sharp-shooter*, accenting *Mango* and *Love pink* feathers on a brightly colored parrot holding a wood sign with "THE" carved in it.

Den's work is next level, a true undiscovered talent.

YaYa and TBS Crew are doing an *intergalactic theme* that is literally out of this world. Three space ships fly one after the other through a meteor shower; each one tagged with part of their crew name, first ship has "THE", second "BOMB", the third and biggest spaceship says "SOCIETY", all in crazy *wild-style* letters.

Riding three meteors are three deep-space aliens, each more bizarre than the next, one even see-through. Yaya's work is unbelievable, even with glaring similarities to Den's, especially the way the bodies are proportioned.

YaYa takes a few sly looks at what tip Den is using, studying his technique. If they were not from opposing crews they might be friends. YaYa doesn't have friends, he has *homies*.

The event DJ spins a new track while a camera crew films it for EnzOne's website and show. He and a group of judges walk amongst the graffiti artists as they paint, taking a look at can control and blending techniques.

EnzOne has done a lot for the graffiti scene; his online show gets over a million views the first twenty-four hours airing. His graffiti shop/café, also called *Planet Street*, is a melting pot of street artists from all over the world who spend far more time there now that he got a beer and wine license than they ever did when it was coffee.

EnzOne's fashion line is also sold in his shop/café and promoted through his website, plus was recently picked up by *Urban Outfitters*. His dream of owning artists' lofts and studios to rent is much closer now. The fame his *Battle-Zone* show has brought to many of the artists has helped them as well, giving them a platform to introduce their talent to millions around the world.

In fact, unbeknownst to Den, he has the biggest following of all. Unfortunately he lives in the stone ages, preferring to not hustle for computers and phones, instead doing so for paint and art supplies.

VENICE BOARD WALK - LUNCH

Electric heat bakes the day as Maple eats a slice of pizza at an outdoor café, boardwalk filled with all walks of life milling about aimlessly. The homeless woman from earlier passes right by her, Dodger's baseball hat pulled low over her eyes, hiding from the day. She approaches some tourists and begs but they ignore her completely. Maple looks down at her table; she has another slice of pizza there. She picks it up and walks from the café, slowly approaching the homeless woman.

The closer Maple gets, the slower she walks, heart pounding in her ears, throat closing up, hands shaking. The woman turns and comes face to face with Maple holding out the pizza.

The woman ponders it, confused—

<u>MAPLE</u>

You can have it if you want.

She gazes right through Maple, as if she isn't even there; she just takes the pizza and walks off eating it. Maple raises her camera, taking a photo of her from behind when she turns, giving Maple a perfectly framed picture of her gaunt, lost face, haunting and drawn.

Maple is frozen inside, uncertain of who she is anymore, not sure of anything all of a sudden. It's like the whole world is caving in, her personality imploding while the universe expands dizzyingly into the infinite beyond her. What is she doing here? What is she looking for? Why is she looking for it?

All Maple knows is life seemed better when she knew her mom was ok, even if she was fucked up and incoherent in her last days living at home, at least she knew she was alive. Never in all her years would she imagine that her beautiful mother, who was brought up in a loving upper-middle-class house hold, who went right into college to study family law, would end up a hopeless, pathetic drug-addict.

Maple's mother met George Baker III while studying law at UCLA and immediately fell in love. He was larger than life, both in personality and stature, also was *very* popular around campus, especially at parties because he always brought *cocaine*.

George is the one who introduced her to cocaine in the first place, so it's all his fault, right? Wrong.

George's personality is different than her mother's, his future prospects were senior to the party, as he became more successful the less he used drugs. On the opposite side of that, her mother used them more and more as her life became secondary to everything else around her.

George would never admit he introduced her mother to narcotics, but Maple remembers her mother stating it very clearly in their last big blow-out. Wasn't long after her mom moved in with her drug dealer, from then on George forbid Maple to see her.

Last year Maple heard her dad mention to a friend that she was in jail for possession, marking the first time Maple tried to find her. She called twelve jails; not one was able to locate her. Then eight months ago while visiting the country club for a family lunch, her mom's old friend laughed about how her mother was *homeless in Venice*.

That night Maple cried herself to sleep like a baby, only wanting to feel her mother's touch, the tickle of her hair when it would brush against her face. *Why was getting high more important than her*, that's all she wanted to know. Maple comes out of her stupor to find the homeless woman nowhere to be seen; just masses of contrasting lives flowing around Maple like water in a great stream sweeping about a protruding stone.

VENICE GRAFFITI WALLS - LATER

The graffiti murals are amazing, TUF Crew's *jungle-scene* versus TBS Crew's *futuristic theme*. The jungle theme is very rich and has a lot of depth, distant mountains show Mayan temples growing from them, funky *amoeba-letters* attached organically to different trees and plants, even oozing over Den's characters.

The *futuristic theme* is incredible, glowing-iridescent lasers fire from cannons projecting out from orbed space-crafts, realistic quality of metal shimmering, finely textured meteors flying through space, strange aliens riding them like wild horses, firing phasors in retaliation, fiery explosions all around them.

The artists stand in front of their art, confidence high in both camps. No graffiti artist takes losing a battle lightly.

EnzOne steps away from one of the tables where the other judges sit, both old-school graffiti artists from Los Angeles. He speaks into a microphone, voice echoing over the sound system—

<u>ENZONE</u>

Lettering style goes to TBS, but it was not an easy decision. Characters on both sides are insane, the backgrounds are phenomenal. We do have one issue to sort out; this is not an easy choice to make for many reasons. *The Unstoppable Force* and *The Bomb Society* have come with it on many levels, can control, shading techniques, lettering styles, all explosive. Only one crew can walk away sponsored by my new line of aerosol paint, *Zone-FX* spray-paint, high and low pressures, dozens of colors.

Den hates it when EnzOne sells himself like an infomercial. Ra and Syne are visibly shaken that their lettering wasn't a *slam-dunk*.

EnzOne confers with the judges.

YaYa and Den eyeball each other, the pressure is on.

Maple walks up and stops at the edge of the crowd, taking in the mind-boggling array of characters surrounding her, this wacky and completely different world than her own, a thrilling, dangerous, unpredictable new galaxy of possibilities with Den at the center.

Den sees Maple; they look longingly at one another, a distance between them not made of space but made of money, made of social class, cultural status, even education. In the real world there isn't a teardrops' chance in *Hades* these two will end up together.

EnzOne steps away from the table once again—

ENZONE

The judges have made a painful decision. TUF Crew held the top spot five months straight. Having won the first and third battles with jungle themes, we decided both pieces are worthy of a win, but due to a lack in originality, this month's battle goes to TBS Crew from North Hollywood. YaYa, you and The Bomb Society will hold the top spot until next month.

TBS Crew celebrates like they won the Super Bowl, these kids don't have much to celebrate, not many people have ever clapped for them or patted them on the back or even wished them a good day, so this is extra special.

TUF Crew sulks away, slowly packing up their gear as Maple approaches cautiously, not sure what this all means.

EnzOne looks to Maple and stops her—

                    ENZONE
        Hey, picture-girl. E-mail those photos
        you took, I'll put 'em on the website,
        give you photo-credit. If they're good
        I'll pay you to photograph the battles.
        Old photographer died last week, big loss
                    for us.

EnzOne hands her a business card.

                    MAPLE
        Really? I'm so sorry. How did he die?

                    ENZONE
        Slammed some laced heroin. Fuckin'
        Fentanyl killin' all kinds of dope-heads.
        He considered himself a classy dope-head,
            now he's a dead dope-head.

                    MAPLE
        That is awful and sad. I'll send you the
        pictures I took, honestly I'm just
        learning about photography in a class I'm
        taking at school. I do love it though.

Den walks up to Maple, just in time to hear the last comment.

                    DEN
        I bet they're amazing, Maple.

                    ENZONE
        Mad skills, Den. Not sure why you went
        jungle theme again, seems like you would
            have tried something more risky.

ENZONE

Sign up for a rematch. You guys have a good shot at getting my sponsorship. Ten cases of *ZoneFX* paint a month for a year.

EnzOne walks off, Den looks at Maple, bummed for the loss but comforted by her presence.

MAPLE

I know you can come back and win that sponsorship, imagine all the amazing murals you can paint when you get it. Maybe you could paint my room? My dad would literally shit himself, likely tear down that whole part of the house.

DEN

I bet I could win him over.

MAPLE

You would have to get new shoes though; he would never let you in the house with those. I love them, I think they're sexy, but he would be worried you would ruin the white rug in the sitting room.

DEN

Sitting room? My entire apartment is a sitting room. I shared a room with my brother until I was thirteen for fuck sake. You have a sibling?

MAPLE

Nope, just me and Rosita.

DEN

Rosita your cat or something?

                         MAPLE

    Noooo, she's our maid. She's worked for
    us since I was two. She's kind of like a
    surrogate mom or live-in grandmother. Our
    household would fall apart without her.

                          DEN

    I'm my own maid. Not a very good one.

Maple smiles—

                         MAPLE

    I know how fortunate I am if that's what
    you're thinking, I don't take anything
    for granted. My dad won't let me anyway,
    he makes me work most weekends at his law
    firm, I told a little *white-lie* to get
            out of it today. Oh, and—

Maple reaches in her bag, giving den
smoothie drink and protein bar.

                         MAPLE

    Almost forgot, these are for you. Heard
          you mention you hadn't eaten.

                          DEN

    I hardly ever eat, except cereal and
                ramen noodles.

Something about Den brings out Maple's
maternal instincts, she just wants to pack him
up and take him home with her. She flutters
her eyes, trying to rid herself of these
overwhelming thoughts.

                         MAPLE

              Walk me to my car?

Den shrugs the affirmative, allowing her to lead him away. Fyre watches, getting jealous in spite of herself.

She walks toward them—

<u>FYRE</u>

Hey Den, we aren't slaves, you know. Could use a little help packing up.

Den stops, feeling an obligation to his crew but also not giving a fuck about any of them right now. Blast comes to the rescue, always a good friend, a best friend actually.

Blast is Den's oldest friend; they met in third grade when Den first moved to Venice from northern California. In sixth grade they pissed on all the toilet seats in the girl's bathroom between classes and got caught. It was truly a bonding moment that will inevitably last a life-time.

Blast was essential in helping Den keep his head on straight after his brother was killed, but even his friendship wasn't enough to keep Den from sinking to a very deep low.

<u>BLAST</u>

I got you, bro, do your thing.

Den *shrugs*, walking away with Maple. It is unarguable, Den and Maple look right together, something about their energies acts as a balancing mechanism between wildly powerful beings. Together they bring the best of both worlds, filling the voids they have in their souls from horrible losses. Together they bring life to a loveless universe filled with a myriad of incalculable distractions.

Blast turns to Fyre—

BLAST

Jealous, Fyre?

FYRE

Whatever, I'm with Casper now.

This news is shocking to Blast. He thought
he knew Fyre pretty well, she has been his
friend longer than Den, but never has she ever
been attracted to gang-bangers, especially
ones like Casper; dude is not attractive and
has the moral compass of *Charles Manson*.

BLAST

Casper? Dude looks like that vulture in
those old Warner Brothers cartoons.

FYRE

You look like a furry brown beach-ball
with legs.

BLAST

You're not with him for the *meth* are you?
Everyone knows he sells that shit.

FYRE

Don't be an idiot. Casper has a totally
different side that none of you will
ever get to see, he's actually really
sweet to me, Blast, so suck hairy balls.

She turns away, glancing at Den and Maple
before they are swallowed by the crowd,
knowing she just told a *bold lie* to Blast.

In reality Casper is an immature, sexist,
bigoted, violent, combative, asshole that only
does what Fyre asks because he's wanted to
bang her since he sprouted his first pubic
hair. Finally got her high enough on Meth to

convince her having sex would be a great idea; that was last week, now they're "dating".

VENICE BOARDWALK - LATER

Den and Maple walk along the boardwalk, he drinks his smoothie and finishes the protein-bar, throwing the trash on the ground. Maple is about to say something but stops herself, instead she takes a manila envelope from her bag and hands it to him.

Den tosses the empty smoothie bottle off to the side and opens the envelope; pulling out the photos she took the first time they met, including the one Den took of Blast. They're really good; Den is very touched by the gesture; a hard shell softens before her eyes.

DEN

No one has ever taken photos of my work like this. That is such a trip now that I think about it.

MAPLE

What's a trip?

DEN

I could never afford a camera. I don't have many photos of my work, you know? I mean ninety-nine percent of my paintings are gone forever, no photos, no canvases, nothing. That's what's a trip about graffiti art, you can't keep it. It's like riding a good wave; you can only enjoy it for so long before it breaks completely, and then you paddle out for a new one, and ride that.

Maple guides him up an alley to a parking-lot. They arrive at her car, her brand new champagne BMW SUV with limo-tint and *blinged-out* Asanti rims.

Before either one can say another word a beat-up rust-grey 80's Coup De Ville pulls up the alley, parking beside them, loud hip-hop bumping gangster-rap from a trunk full of speakers. You can even hear the metal car frame rattle with every drop of the 808 bass.

Den's head sags as Casper, Sueno and two more cholos from C-13 step out, approaching with menace.

Maple tenses, almost turning to run, but Den clutches her arm protectively, letting her know she is safe.

CASPER

What's up, ranker? How's your brother?

Casper bumps shoulders with Den, knocking his sunglasses from his hand. Casper steps on his shades, splintering them in a thousand tiny pieces like *Mickey Mouse* did to his broomstick in *"Fantasia"*.

The gangsters laugh, walking toward the boardwalk. Maple is dumbfounded, not sure how to react or if she should react, by the looks of it, Den isn't reacting much.

It takes every ounce of control Den can muster not to say something back to them.

MAPLE

Who are they?

DEN

No one worth talking about.

He watches them walk away, silently pissed.

                          MAPLE

                How old is your brother?

Den just shrugs, not wanting to talk about
it and Maple doesn't want to push it.

                          DEN

                This is your car?

                         MAPLE

     My dad says it's the safest, won't let me
              drive anything less.

                          DEN

          Wow. Must care for you a lot.

                         MAPLE

            Sometimes way too much.

                          DEN

      You can never care for your kids too
                        much.

They think about that, examining each other
closely, recording every twitch, each movement
of the eye, absently drifting away in a field
of infinite possibilities. Maple blushes,
unlocking her car with an abrasively loud
chirp sounding out an end to this magical day.

Maple opens the door and stares at her car
seat like she expects it to do something.

Den creases his eyes curiously—

                         MAPLE

                You busy later?

He shrugs, that's his specialty, shrugging.
Den has mastered the art of *the shrug*,
developing specific shrugs for every occasion;

each shrug carrying a volume of meaning, and *this shrug* says he would do anything she asks of him for the rest of his life.

Maple takes a print out of the *E-vite* she got for her best friend's party from her car and hands it to him.

MAPLE

Come see me tonight. My best friend Jessica's birthday party, it's a Hawaiian theme. You don't have to dress up.

DEN

Maybe.

MAPLE

That isn't an acceptable answer.

DEN

These are the only shoes I have and a toe starting to poke through, which isn't Hawaiian at all.

MAPLE

Like I said, your shoes are sexy.

Maple's confidence is jarring, almost makes Den want to run away. I mean, really? This chick and Den? He isn't buying they have a chance but desperately wants to believe they do.

DEN

If I can get a ride, I'll roll through.

MAPLE

I didn't even think about that, I am such a dunce. Ummm, I *can't* come and get you, otherwise I swear I would. She's my bestie. I have to be there before the party starts for family stuff.

                    MAPLE

    If you can't make it, we can, I don't
know, meet at a Starbucks or something. I
         can drive down to see you.

                     DEN

    That's cool, all good, I mean… Bel Air? I
     don't even know if that's real to me.

                    MAPLE

    Oh, do you want my number? Or I'll just
    call you about all the pictures from
    today, if you want them. I took so many.
       Happy to bring some more to you.

                     DEN

              Sure, if you want.

                    MAPLE

                 I do want.

    You can almost hear the electricity
crackling in the air.

                     DEN

       Later, Maple-like-the-syrup.

                    MAPLE

       Later, Den-short-for-Dennis.

    Den slowly backs off, finding it hard to
disengage from this diamond, this rare jewel,
this priceless gem. He drops his skate and
pushes off down the alley, not looking back.

    Maple struggles with her feelings, sure that
he was going to look back but he doesn't.
Crestfallen she starts to get in her car when,
like magic, he does. Right before rolling out
of view he catches one last look back, locking
eyes one final time. The connection so

powerful it is as if he is standing only inches away from her.

Maple smiles, warmed from within. This makes no sense whatsoever but feels so right.

STREETS OF VENICE - DAY

Den skates along, doing tricks all the way, pumped up, invigorated with a new sense of hope for the future. He power-slides to a stop, takes out a *Uni-wide* marker with purple *Grog Ink*, tagging 'Den Maple' on a bus stop.

Even if Maple is just symbolic of future possibilities she represents a change for the better, a shift in consciousness toward a deeper relationship with life, something Den has not had in a very long time.

He kick-flips, camel-flips, bubble-flips, disco-flips, and back-side heal-flips; he blunt slides, barley-grinds, tail-slides, lips-slides off anything and everything, ending in a rail-slide down a narrow stairwell right into the street where a car skids to a stop in a cloud of burnt rubber and hot breaks, barely missing Den.

But he doesn't flinch; doesn't even get an adrenaline rush.

Life for Den has been one of many let-downs. Not so often has he been close to some semblance of normalcy, when those rare moments arose they were always dashed to pieces by some uncontrollable turn of events. His memory of having no fears of money was during his darkest days after his brother died.

Den chose to escape the pain with drugs and alcohol, in order to fuel his addiction he stole anything he could and sold the drugs he was using. It wasn't long before he had enough

money to pay his mother's rent for several
months, which she reluctantly accepted.

But all good things come to an end,
especially when they are based on lies.

DEN'S APARTMENT - LATE DAY

Den skateboards up to his apartment and
walks upstairs. He remembers when he was young
that it was the nicest place they ever lived,
but as he grew older, so did the look of the
building. Now he knows it's a shit-hole and
always was a shit-hole.

He has eleven neighbor's, three are old as
the *Bible*, an ancient black man and two
elderly white women, on Friday nights the
three of them sometimes get drunk and play
dominos. Other patrons of this fine
establishment are a Hindu taxi driver who is
rarely seen, three low-wage Mexican families
with more kids than you can count, a fat
tattoo artist and his girlfriend, surfer in
his sixties that always hits on his mom, plus
cocaine addicted used car salesman and
security guard from the local *Vons*.

Den knows and ignores them all.

When he reaches his door he stops, listening
intently... Is that his mother crying? Den leans
his ear toward the door; it is definitely his
mother crying. He can't decide if he should go
in or not. Bad news right now would be
terrible. Den is still riding the pink cloud
of potential love and God-forbid it should be
soiled by some bad news. He looks down at his
paint covered shoes, pinky toe showing
through. He wiggles it a little, thinking
hard.

After a quiet moment he gets his key out and
plugs it in, turning the lock; the crying

stops. As he enters, he sees his mom hurry into her bedroom. Den closes the front door and re-locks it as his mother closes her bedroom door.

Den stands there a moment, wind taken from his sails, thinking once again, so close to something that makes him feel normal and alive, an event that is out of his control shall come to pass and ruin it. Den breaths deep and goes to her bedroom, knocking—

> DEN

> Mom?

He hears sounds of shuffling, a drawer closing, clink of glass, her cracking voice—

> CONNIE'S VOICE

> I'm alright, Denny.

Den rests his head against the door, wishing he could save her, wishing he could save himself. He hears her weep quietly decides to open the door finding her face down on the bed not looking up.

> DEN

> Tell me.

> CONNIE

> It's not your problem. You shouldn't have to worry about it.

> DEN

> About what?

Connie holds back sobs, shoulders quaking with emotion. Den shuffles over to her and sits on the edge of the bed. Watching her a

moment, he lowers himself beside her, hugging
her protectively, letting her insulating layer
dissipate, true feelings unfolding.

<u>DEN</u>

I love you, mom. Everything will be ok.

Connie cries, not able to stop this one,
it's bad, something is very bad for her,
another great blow from the trickster god;
some new grave unsettling occurrence is making
itself known.

CHAPTER FIVE - DIE REICHEN KINDER
JESSICA'S BEDROOM - NIGHT

Jessica Pollard, Maple 's best friend since second grade, sits in a white-suede lounge chair in her massive personal suite at the family's Bel Air mansion, half dressed for her upcoming birthday party.

Jessica has thick brunette hair, face mousy-cute with an athletic build. She's never been sad in her life, not *really* sad. No one has died that she loves, she's never had her electricity turned off, never been evicted, always eaten organic, never had a bad grade, never been suspended, never heard her parents fight, never ate McDonald's because she *had* to, always has money in her purse, never been broke, never met a poor person, never been to the hood, never will go to the hood.

Her father is founder and CEO of RADIOQUIP, the largest provider of radiology equipment on planet Earth, his net-worth is over 1.3 Billion and growing.

The other two besties kick-back on a matching white-suede sofa. Carly is a spicy, audacious red-head, gangly as a giraffe and tells everyone she will be a Victoria's Secret model one day, which she is on her way to being dressed like she is tonight. Her parents are happily divorced surgeons, but the divorce forced Carly out of Bel Air to Brentwood, a tragic step-down.

Tiff is a trendy Afro-American teen whose father is a music mogul from the nineties;

she's their groups gate-way to the stars. Tiff
grew up hanging out with a *menu* of A-list
celebrities as long as *Santa's Christmas list.*

They look at pictures of Den at the graffiti
battle posted to Maple's *Instagram,* focusing
on a close up of Den; green, pink, and black
paint splatter is drizzled across his glowing
expression, emerald-eyes inset perfectly, tiny
shade of man's first beard shadowing his
etched jaw-line.

The girls swoon—

TIFF

He's totally hot. Those eyes...

Tiff melts with curiosity as Maple comes out
of the bathroom, hair in curlers, make-up
half-finished. Jessica looks up from her
phone, concerned for her bestie, agreeing he
is handsome but credentials are less credible.

JESSICA

I can't believe you invited him.

MAPLE

Why?

JESSICA

Ummm, besides the obvious? I mean, sure
he's cute and mysterious, but come on,
really? He doesn't even have a cellphone.
How are you going to date him without a
cellphone? Plus, helloooooooo, duh? Grant?
Your super-jealous ex-bf? He'll lose his
shit and beat him up.

MAPLE

I'm pretty sure Den can defend himself,
and I'm not dating him, I invited him to
a stupid party.

Jessica gives her an offended look, like--
'My party, stupid?'

                    MAPLE

            You know what I mean.

                    CARLY

        Does he have any friends? I like bad
              boys. Are they poor?

                    MAPLE

            Are you kidding?

Carly's not, her look says so. Tiff tries on
some of Jessica's clothes from the walk-in
closet, making a mess.

                    MAPLE

        I haven't the slightest idea if they're
                  poor, Carly.

Maple knows Den is poor; in her deepest
imaginings the likelihood she makes a fair
comparison of his experience with anything she
could relate to is still slim at best.

                    CARLY

        Call him. Make sure he's coming.

                    MAPLE

        I don't know. Maybe. He didn't seem
        excited about the invite when I gave it
                    to him.

Tiff steps once again from the closet in a
plush deep-purple sweater, she caresses it
seductively—

                    TIFF

        Oh my god, this *cashmere*? I love it.

Jessica and Carly toss their phones aside
and join Tiff in the closet, excited about the
sweater she found.

Omg, I haven't seen this sweater in like...
two months. I got it in Aspen at this
French boutique, my dad paid like eight-
hundred for it which is a great deal.

Maple stares at them, lost in her own
moment, suddenly outcast from her group,
suddenly at odds with her own certainty. Maybe
this has all been a huge mistake, I mean, she
only just met this kid, who knows what he's
really like.

What about the gang-bangers that scared her
and that creepy guy Yaya from the valley? Who
is this Den person? What the hell is she
thinking?

Maple looks back at a photo of Den on her
Instagram, just looking at his image on a
digital screen makes her feel like he is right
there in the room with her, like she can touch
him. None of it makes sense, does it have to?

Maple wasn't raised to define herself by
relationships; she was raised to define
herself by her own accomplishments. Her
greatness must come senior to anything else;
her future must take first place before anyone
or anything. She was trained to ignore
children or marriage, to concern herself with
success and legend.

George Baker III raised Maple Baker to be
self-reliant and to treat love as a lesser
life-impediment. Not her mother, all she
wanted was love. George loved the *idea* of her,
loved her in a bikini on a yacht party, loved
her when they were wasted together, but in

normal every-day life, he didn't really love her the way she wanted. She was a ghost haunting well decorated halls of a multi-million dollar home, a lunatic in an insane asylum of her own making.

Maple's mother could have done anything she wanted in life; she had a law degree, she was a semi-pro tennis player, she was smart and gorgeous, spoke three languages, yet all she wanted in the end was to get high and *stay high*. Now she's gone, lost to the very streets that Den knows so well. Maybe that's why she longs for Den, because she longs for her mother and hopes upon hope that her mother, deep inside, longs for her too.

CHAPTER SIX - LOS NINOS POBRES

STREETS OF VENICE - NIGHT

A street-light flickers rhythmically over well tagged side-walks and walls, Cyclones, C-Trece, Cyclones Thirteen, C-13, Cyclones Trece written all over. Traffic is sparse in this out-cast enclave of Venice where gangs still hold down territory and most houses sold get torn down. A Latino community with block after block of run-down apartments slowly deteriorating with each passing day.

Den skates around a corner, coming down a small street where numerous cars try to find parking. Loud music comes from a shit-hole corner-house up the road.

Den, headphones on, skates down the street when Casper's 80's Coup De Ville whips past him, its' side-view mirror clipping Den's hip, spinning him off his board.

He tumbles to a dreadful stop, hearing the rattle of metal and an 808 bass.

Casper drives over a curb and parks right in the grass on the front lawn of the house. Teenagers and young adults hang about outside slowly making their way into the party.

Den lays there in the middle of the road for a moment, clutching his knee and elbow, wincing through the soreness, his skateboard still rolling up the street ahead.

He sits up, catches a few people laughing as they pass, shakes it off and rises, limping toward his skateboard, feeling like a chump.

Grabbing his board from the ground he heads around the side of the house instead of front where Casper and his ghouls hover.

Over a six-foot cinder-block wall, multi-colored lights flash accompanied by loud industrial-house music and a cacophony of voices all blending together in a mad mixture of certain mayhem.

Den balances his skateboard on the wall and hops over with ease, dropping into the freak-show beyond.

BLAST'S HOUSE - NIGHT

The backyard is mostly dirt with a few tufts of shrubbery, except for a huge Rusty Leaf Fig tree growing in the middle, dense branches stretch over the party, bushy leaves creating a mighty canopy above them. Its' botanical name is *Ficus rubiginosa* and tolerates salt-spray conditions well, making it an optimum choice for beach communities, very common in the area.

Den grabs his skate from the wall, taking it all in.

Every available bit of wall space on the interior cinder-block is covered in TUF Crew graffiti-art. Den scans the pieces, all of them so fresh, but none of them have his lettering, just his characters.

A large, rundown quarter-pipe that has seen it's better days sits against the back wall, Blast and Syne skate the pipe doing basic tricks, a fifty-fifty grind, a fakie, nothing special, while Ra-One tokes on a bong and critiques them.

Funny that Ra tells them what they are doing right or wrong when he doesn't even skate himself. But that's Ra for you, a selfish prick.

Ra moved to Venice from the Inland Empire where TUF Crew started back in the nineties. Ra thinks because his brother was one of the original five members and since he started the Venice chapter four years ago that *he* is the alpha and omega on how things go down. In fact they're the last five members *in* TUF Crew, most dropped the clique when Ra rubbed them the wrong way too many times. Only reason Den and Blast stick around is because Fyre and Ra are cousins and they're best friends with her.

But that's what gave birth to *UnKnown Artists*, so it can't be all bad. Case was so tired of hearing Den and Blast complain about Ra not letting them paint what *they* wanted, he suggested starting their own crew, but not tell anyone. Stay completely unknown but get up really hard, create a *great urban mystery* where nothing once existed.

Case had wanted to start painting again; none of his homies from Ghost Town Crips are into bombing, so he even keeps it secret from them. Plus it gives Case and Den something creative to do together, since Case introduced his brother to gang-life he feels complicate in his murder, a morbid guilt that runs deep.

The party is just getting started; Den can see people are already pretty wasted as unforgiving wafts of marijuana smoke drift about the crowd like some nuclear aftermath. Through the smoggy-haze of dancing lights he sees Fyre at her DJ set up spinning records, really into it. This is her passion; her future is being a famous DJ spinning at huge events like *Burning Man, Sunburn Fest, Electric Daisy Carnival,* or *Tomorrowland.*

Fyre's DJ equipment is pretty fucking professional considering she's only in high-school. Fyre is broke too, but not the kind of broke Den is, Den is the kind of broke that is broke by third-world standards, not even bordering on doing anything in America.

Fyre has always had a legit job ever since she was twelve when her dad opened an ice-cream shop on the Venice Boardwalk, which is still there today but no longer owned by her father. He's serving fifteen to twenty years in prison for narcotics distribution, his ice-cream shop sold by the courts for laundering drug money through it.

Den was sure her dad's ice-cream joint was a hit because all summer it would be absolutely packed with customers, having no idea Fyre's pop was running fake receipts to clean his drug-money.

Den never had a clue Fyre's dad was supplying C-13 with most of the dope they were slanging. Since her dad's been in prison, Fyre's mom lost the house, cars, jewelry, pets, almost everything they owned and now live in a one bedroom apartment, her mom sleeping in the living-room. Fyre spends a lot of time alone, in fact it's been fourteen days since she saw her mother last.

Her and Den's mom used to be *road-dogs* when they were younger, Den certain they met while working as strippers near LAX. Connie insists only Fyre's mom was a stripper, that she only served drinks, but Den is suspicious.

Fyre's mom is clean from drugs and alcohol for two years, spending most of her time at her sober boyfriend's place who used to be a stockbroker but now drives Uber.

Den hates the days their parents hung-out, his mom was with a lot of different guys back then, that just pissed he and his brother off. On at least three occasions they got in physical altercations with guys she brought home. He understood she was lonely and had lousy taste in men, coupled with a drinking problem is a recipe for disaster.

One thing good that came out of all of it, Fyre's mom bought her everything she needs to be a DJ while they still had some money, now she gets paid to DJ at house parties and small raves, so she must be doing something right. That and she's really good at it.

Fyre finally sees Den across the yard; she gives him a pithy nod then goes back to her music as Blast's older brother Trey-dog staggers by with a surfing buddy. T-Dog is a long-haired-lanky-Mexican-hard-core-surfer who loves to argue about how best to squeeze into a small tube whilst surfing; how to *best thread the needle* so to speak. He's a pretty shitty surfer to be honest.

Den wanders through the crowd like he's invisible, meeting up with his crew at the quarter-pipe. Ra puffs heavy on the bong, blowing smoke everywhere—

RA-ONE

Yo, Den... You fuckin cheesed on them characters, dog.

Ra hops down from the quarter-pipe and walks away in a huff, joining a few other writers by some rusty lawn furniture, handing them the bong. Blast kicks his board away, walking to Den, Syne continues doing tricks behind them; a tail-grab here, boneless there.

                    BLAST

    Don't listen to Ra, bro, he's butt-hurt
        'cause he blew the theme.

                     DEN

    Whatever, man, this is bullshit. Fuck
                    this.

                    BLAST

      What's that supposed to mean?

                     DEN

    Beats the shit outta me, Blast, I just
    know something has to change for me or
       I'm gonna to blow a gasket.

                    BLAST

    I feel you, but shit ain't changing
              tonight so…

    Blast shrugs 'whatever' and Den answers him
    with his own 'shrug of agreement'.

                     DEN

     Oh yeah, cops got a picture of you in
                   action.

    Den takes the picture of Blast Maple gave
    him from his backpack.

                    BLAST

     Keep that shit bro, I hate me in
               pictures,

                     DEN

    You do look like a *Mexican Ralphie May*.

    Blast heads of—

BLAST

Ha-ha. I'm-a grab a beer.

Den puts the picture away as he slowly navigates over toward Fyre, stepping around behind the DJ set-up so he is close to her.

She knows he is there but ignores him—

DEN

How you doin', Fyre?

Fyre pretends she can't hear him through the headphones but Den knows she can. Den shakes his head about to walk away when she pulls her headphones down and looks at him.

FYRE

You say something?

Den shakes his head 'no' and goes back to being a wall-flower. Fyre watches him from the corner of her eye as she goes back to mixing, ignoring the huge mistake she feels she made by breaking up with him, I mean what was she supposed to do?

Den stopped partying and didn't want to be around drugs anymore and, well, Fyre likes a little Meth every now and then, definitely likes weed or vodka. It was for Den's own protection she broke up with him, after-all, Den was on probation, going to Narcotics Anonymous meetings, he was sober! Fuck that, Fyre is seventeen, way too young to be sober.

Fyre never thought of herself as having a drug problem anyway, at least not yet. Since she currently has to pay her own way through life, dating Casper is a plus since; A, he

always has extra money for food or whatever,
and; B, he gives her free Meth when she wants.

Den starts toward the quarter-pipe where
Syne is still at it, possessed, he bails on a
front-side-air, skidding to a splintery stop.

Blast rejoins Den with a full cup of beer—

                    BLAST

   Syne is on Mali bro, dude is twisted.

They watch Syne roll around like a Python
rolling up a baby pig, laughing to himself.

                    DEN

      Wanna roll out with me?

                    BLAST

                  Where?

Fyre walks up, letting a track play for a
while. She takes Blast's beer and drinks it
against his will.

                    DEN

        Big party in Bel Air.

                    BLAST

   That photography-chick invite you? Homie
   she is fine, dude, like I ain't seen no
   shit like that. Maybe on TV, like those
   Disney Channel shows, she looks like she
   could be on one of those shows, is she?
   Wouldn't surprise me if she was, I don't
   watch 'em anymore, least not that you
                  fools know.

Fyre smolders with jealousy but plays it
off. Den hands him the flyer Maple gave him—

                    FYRE

   Gonna be some rich-ho's for ya, Blast.

<u>BLAST</u>

You just said the magic-words; *rich-ho's.*

Fyre looks at Den, peeved.

<u>FYRE</u>

Got a little sugar-momma, Den?

<u>DEN</u>

Don't worry about it, no sweat off your
back.

<u>BLAST</u>

You know her and Casper hooked up.

Den is frozen in disbelief then shakes his
head, completely blown away by that.

<u>DEN</u>

Dating a gang-banger? That's smart.

<u>FYRE</u>

Don't talk shit. You wanted freedom, you
got it.

<u>DEN</u>

Ummm... You dumped me.

<u>FYRE</u>

Only 'cause you wanted me too.

<u>DEN</u>

That makes a lot of sense.

Den looks away from Fyre to Syne who still
rolls around on the skate ramp, dusted.

<u>DEN</u>

We should break, Blast. If you're down.

BLAST

My brother's parties end in disaster
anyway, fuck it. How we getting there?

Den's *shrug* suggests not to worry. Fyre
notices—

FYRE

Don't hang out with Case. Cyclones find
out, you're dust.

DEN

Then don't tell them.

Fyre loves Den so much but ego won't let
her follow heart. Blast grabs his skateboard
following Den to the cinderblock wall but
Blast stops him.

BLAST

I got a gate, dude.

Fyre watches Blast pull Den to a gate by the
corner of his house, she waits for Den to look
back, but he doesn't.

Casper, Sueno and several other Cyclones
enter the backyard from the main house. Casper
looks at Fyre, smiling his crooked smile he
blows her a kiss.

She reluctantly smiles back, knowing this
choice is doomed to failure, Meth or no Meth,
Casper is a horrible person; he has stabbed
people, beaten people, shot at people, all for
a kid of seventeen. What a loser.

Fyre's shoulders sag, she heads to her DJ
set-up leaving Syne flopping around behind her
on the quarter-pipe.

VENICE STREETS - NIGHT

Den and Blast walk down the street, holding
their boards. Den seems down and distant,
silently bummed. Blast can feel it, they know
each-other so well, they have each-others'
back no doubt.

BLAST

You alright?

DEN

My mom got fired today.

Blast shakes his head, that's some very
heavy news.

BLAST

What are you going to do?

Den *shrugs*, uncertain.

DEN

She's got extra shifts bartending for
Tommy-Tom, but I just don't want her
working in those places, you know? Plus
Tommy is fuckin' degenerate.

BLAST

Tell her to call Fyre's mom. She's sober.

Den sits on a short wall covered in C-13
graffiti, *numb as a cadaver.*

DEN

Older I get, more wack life gets. It's a
bad trip.

Blast looks at the ground, knowing exactly
what he means. Life has not been easy for

Blast either, but his parents are still together, and they do own a house, a shitty house, but at least it's a house.

Blast's parents are difficult, to put it lightly. His father owns his own machine-shop in Culver City, does a lot of work for the movie business at times, but he is very religious and usually very drunk.

His mom doesn't speak any English at all and they mismanage their finances like children. Since they purchased a small house in San Francisquito, the small town his mother's family is from on the east coast of the Baja Peninsula, they haven't been around much.

The "vacation" home is also a shit-hole, but it is beautiful down there, in fact Blast secretly wants to abandon his dreams of being a comic-book artist and move there after high-school to open some kind of bullshit-business. He hasn't told anyone about this, he knows they would think it was stupid.

The low thump of an 808 bass kick is followed by the metallic rattle of a car-frame.

<u>BLAST</u>

That better not be Casper, dude.

<u>DEN</u>

Fuck Casper.

<u>BLAST</u>

Don't say that, bro, don't even think it.

A lowered, Prince-purple VW Bug with an airbrushed painting of a skeleton climbing out of a grave holding a cane with a blue bandana tied to the end, a painting Den's brother did four years ago. Ornate black pin-striping streaks down the sides while neon-purple low-profile lights glow from underneath.

The psychedelic-beetle pulls up to the curb, Case driving—

CASE

Let's roll big-homies!

Hydraulics hiss and the car lowers to the ground. They get in, hydraulics spitting, car raising, Case peals out leaving a thick plume of burnt rubber wafting the street.

CAPTER SEVEN - DARK NIGHT COMETH
BEL AIR MANSION - NIGHT

Jessica's mansion is big as a building, four stories of ultra-modern architecture, eighteen thousand square-feet of state-of-the-art interior living space, plus a full acre of land sprawling out in all directions; entire house lit up like the *Princess' Castle at Disney Land.*

All manner of expensive cars fill the parking-lot sized driveway as teenagers create an upward avalanche of bodies cascading towards the party beyond; it's loud and obnoxious, rich and spoiled, but other-wise a great time.

The low thump of 808 bass and metallic-rattle of a car frame draws everyone's attention to Case's Prince-purple VW pulling up the steep driveway, luminous purple-neon radiating off the black-top.

People are obviously annoyed but politely move out of the way, curious as hell about the unknown intruders. Many laugh and point at the ridiculousness of his car, they wouldn't be caught dead in something like that.

CASE'S VW BUG - SAME TIME

The music is way too loud, that added to the fluorescent lights glowing on the interior too; make it rather gaudy and other-worldly indeed. The three of them watch out the windows like fish in a bowl, none of them feeling exactly comfortable here but all are down to experience something different, something classy, something they may never experience again.

Case lights a blunt, puffing madly, filling the car with smoke, Den leans away from it trying not to breath.

CASE

Gotta get out the car in puff of smoke.

BLAST

Maybe we should have just parked down below, you know? Just walked up like everyone else.

CASE

Hell, no. You go to a nice restaurant, you valet.

Case puffs away, passing the blunt to Blast who happily takes it.

DEN

No fucking around tonight, alright? Best behavior. Don't fuck this up.

CASE

We'll be choir-boys, cuz. I even put on some dress clothes for this shindig.

BLAST

That's a button-up shirt and some new Dickies, bro.

CASE

This is my penguin-suit, get used to it.

FRONT OF MANSION - MOMENTS LATER

Case pulls to a stop, blocking in two BMW's, one of them is Maple's. The hydraulics spit, VW lowering to the ground. The teens look at the spectacle, some intrigued, others disgusted.

Case opens his door in a huge cloud of smoke as Den and Blast get out the other side. Everyone stares at them as if they were aliens emerging from that flying-saucer in the original *"War of the Worlds"*.

                    CASE

Now this is what I call a party!

JESSICA'S BEDROOM - SAME TIME

Jessica, Maple, Carly, Tiff and a few other well-dressed girls gather around the window, looking down at the driveway, the smoke from Case's car still slowly dissipating above the Prince-purple VW Bug.

                    TIFF

Oh my god! Can you believe that car? How
                   ghetto!

                   CARLY

              It's cute.

                  JESSICA

That Den guy is way hotter in person.

Down below, Den looks around, uncomfortable.

                   MAPLE

        I know... He turns me on...

                    TIFF

I'm so pretending you didn't just say
that, I'm officially disgusted. You would
     have to pay for every meal.

The bedroom door bursts open, they jump and squeal, completely startled. Maple's ex-boyfriend, Grant Perkins, barges in with three of his lacrosse playing buddies dressed in Hawaiian shirts, pissed—

<u>MAPLE</u>

You scared the crap out of us, Grant! Knock or something. Have some decency.

Grant is super athletic and chiseled from ancient Grecian marble, the all-American perfect guy and a total dick. He is extremely well educated and well groomed; parents of the best stock, both come from prominent, wealthy California families.

His father's family was part of the *California Gold-Rush* in 1849, but they got into textiles instead of mining, ending up in San Francisco where they invested in an import-export company which is now the biggest on the west coast, having active operations in every port of entry from San Diego to Seattle.

Grant's mother's family earned their first fortune with six thousand acres of almond groves out in the California desert back in the 1930's, using that money to develop a line of non-perishable food products which they sold to the military making billions off WWII, Korean War, Vietnam War, Gulf Wars I and II, the war in Afghanistan, and every skirmish or military deployment in between.

Grant's father got in on the almond game for fun after Grant's mom insisted that he couldn't do anything lucrative with almonds, so in the early 1990's he invested some of *his* family's money into *her* family's original business and starting a line of organic almond milk, building it into the largest selling brand world-wide.

He has no reason to be a dick, parents are both really sweet, but his young ego always feels under attack, the competition amongst the wealthy class to be the richest in the room is fierce. A competition he doesn't take lightly.

He also doesn't take lightly being dumped by the most prude girl in school, after-all he *is* known as *the cherry-popper* and isn't about to let Maple's *cherry* get away.

Maple never really liked him in the first place; she dated him because Jessica was dating his best friend, so it just made it easier for them all to hang out.

Besides, Maple barely let Grant touch her boobs and hated making-out with him, he was horrible at it.

GRANT

Who the hell is that?!

Maple isn't sure what to say, looking to the others for an answer. No one has one.

GRANT

Did you invite that gutter trash to Jessica's birthday? That is fucking rude and childish.

JESSICA

I told her to invite him, Grant.

GRANT

Bullshit, I know you better than that, you don't want those dirt-bags leaving fleas all over.

                        CARLY
        Have you always been this much of a jerk?

    Grant just fumes, they look out the window,
Den and his friends are gone, only the Prince-
purple VW Bug is left. A small crowd has even
gathered around Case's car as locals laugh and
point.

                        GRANT
        White trash better not be inside.

    He and his buddies stomp out of the room,
puffing up like angry *kangaroos*. Jessica
silently pleads with Maple to *do something* as
the girls follow them out of the room.

BEL AIR MANSION - NIGHT
    Jessica's mansion is filled with party-
goers, dressed in expensive fashions, many in
the Hawaiian theme. The house in minimalist
and extremely sexy; a sure-fire *panty-dropper*.
    Den, Case, and Blast make their way past
watchful eyes, taking in their new
surroundings like the first Pilgrims stepping
off the gang-plank of the Mayflower. Den leans
over to his friends—

                        DEN
        I feel like an alien species.

                        BLAST
        Should we bounce?

                        CASE
        Chill, have fun. We're cool.

106

Den shrugs, Blast smiles at a couple of hot rich girls, they're disgusted and their boyfriends are pissed.

UPSTAIRS HALLWAY - SAME TIME

Grant heads down the hall with his buddies, brute determination on his face. Maple tries to stop him, grabbing his arm, her girlfriends right behind her, Jessica totally panicking.

MAPLE

Grant! He's just a friend, you're acting crazy.

GRANT

You don't know crazy. They think they can roll up here like they own the place?! I didn't even get to park up front.

They reach an over-sized, steel beam staircase; Grant yanks his arm away and continues downstairs.

MAPLE

That is so lame! Why are you being like this?!

GRANT

I'm not being like anything, I'm just taking the trash out.

Grant's buddies laugh as they reach the bottom of the stairs and enter into the throngs of party-goers.

JESSICA

Do something, Maple! This is your fault. Omg, my party is going to be ruined!

The girls follow after, people in the crowd are starting to notice the drama and follow them out back.

MANSION BACK YARD - MOMENTS LATER

The backyard is decorated like a Hawaiian fantasy land, tiki torches, grass huts, traditional *hula-dancers* shimmy in front of a high-end DJ system under a gazebo, speakers bump hip-hop so loud the water in the pool shakes. There are even open bars that serve alcohol, Case can't believe his fucking eyeballs, sensory overload too much to handle.

The three graffiti artists end up near the pool's edge, pool itself glowing in a myriad of soft colors, changing from green to blue to red to purple and on through every other color in the rainbow.

CASE

This party is insane, cuz. Blast, you want a drink? They got free fuckin' bars serving alcohol, cuz, what the fuck? That is some pimp shit right there.

BLAST

Yeah, I'll drink whatever.

Case walks to a bar to get a drink, Den and Blast catch people scooting away from them.

DEN

I feel like a retard.

BLAST

Where's your girl?

Den looks around, spotting her walking up—

<u>DEN</u>

Map--

Out of nowhere Den is shoved hard in the
chest by Grant; he damn near tumbles in the
pool but Blast catches him, helping him.

<u>DEN</u>

What's your prob, bro?

<u>GRANT</u>

You mean my prob-lem? There are three
more letters in that word, bum-trash.

Maple pushes her way to Den, standing in
between them, her friends joining, mortified.

<u>DEN</u>

Who is this guy, Maple?

<u>GRANT</u>

I'm her boyfriend, punk.

<u>MAPLE</u>

Ex-boyfriend. I am so sorry, Den.

<u>DEN</u>

Not your fault he's an asshole.

Maple knows that was the wrong thing to say,
so does Blast.

<u>GRANT</u>

Asshole? Speak louder, *skater-boy*, unless
you're scared you'll get knocked out.
Want to get knocked out, *white-trash*? In
Bel Air we don't leave garbage out, it's
clean here, trash doesn't belong, so take
yourself out or I will.

Den shakes his head; this is the very last
thing he wanted.

DEN

Knew this wasn't a good idea.

GRANT

Rich and poor don't mix so take your
dirty ass to the hood.

CASE

Hey rich-boy!

Grant turns in time for Case to throw a
drink in his face.

CASE

We like everyone a little dirty.

Grant immediately throws a wild punch toward
Case which he easily ducks; he doesn't fight
back, just keeps dodging punches—

CASE

I don't want to fuck you up, cuz.

One of Grant's friends sucker punches Case
on the side of the head, giving Grant a moment
to lay one on Case's jaw, all that does is
make Case angrier.

Den, and Blast quickly jump in, Blast laying
out the dude that sucker-punched Case and Den
punching Grant hard in the kidney, dropping
him to a knee.

JESSICA

STOP IT! THIS IS *MY* BIRTHDAY PARTY!

But it's too late for stopping. More of Grant's friends join in, overwhelming Den, Blast, and Case. Den artfully ducks fists, clocking several rich-boys with *stinging jabs*.

MAPLE

Den! Noooo, Den!

Blast is tackled by a gigantic football-playing jock, several other jocks kick him once he's down. Case knocks a guy out, sending him crashing into a bar, bottles and glass break everywhere. Jessica now bouncing in a panic, cellphone *in her hand*, screams—

JESSICA

SOMEONE CALL THE POLICE!

It's total pandemonium; kids are knocked in the pool, lawn-chairs fly through the air, a few jocks grab tiki torches, swinging them at Case who swats them away.

CASE

LET'S FUCKIN' BREAK, YO!

Den and Blast fight their way to Case, Blast socking a *tiki-wielders* causing him to drop his torch on some lawn cushions, bursting into flames. Maple grabs them, tossing the flaming pillows in the pool with a sizzle.

Grant, now back on his feet, grabs Den from behind, pulling him to the ground. Grant and his boys try their best to stomp Den out but Case and Blast punch their way through the football team, grab Den, and run.

Den, Case, and Blast run through the crowd to a wall blocking the back from the front.

                            CASE

          You better jump your fat ass over this
                       wall, Blast.

                           BLAST

               Oh-fuck-oh-fuck-oh-fuck!

     Grant and half the party are behind them
now, near twenty guys, all of them steaming
mad. Maple is paralyzed, never having
experienced anything like this in her life.

     Case and Den are over the wall in seconds;
when Blast jumps he slaps against the wall
like a pancake, arms struggling as twenty guys
barrel down like a *Viking horde*.

     Blast's sneakers squeak against the
concrete, scrambling to escape. At the final
moment, Blast conjures just enough adrenaline
to pull his baby-faced largess over the wall.

     Half the horde climbs in pursuit, others
cutting through the house to the driveway.
Maple sees this and runs for the house with
Jessica, Tiff, and Carly, terrified.

     This night goes down in history as the
wildest night any of these kids has ever had,
it will be talked about for years.

MANSION DRIVEWAY - MOMENTS LATER

     Den, Case, and Blast come from around the
house, sprinting toward the VW, other guys
they haven't seen before start closing in on
them; it's going quickly from twenty against
three to fifty.

     Case gets his door open as Grant and the
others finally catch up. Blast jumps in the
front-seat of the car instead of the back,
making it impossible for Den to squeeze in.

112

Grant and his rich-boys catch Den off-guard, dragging him away from the car where they throw as many punches and kicks as humanly possible.

<u>BLAST</u>

DEN!!! CASE, THEY GOT DEN!!!

Maple, Jessica and others arrive out front; Maple nearly collapses when she sees Den getting beaten.

<u>JESSICA</u>

My party is totally ruined!

Blast dives into the fray, throwing hay-makers left and right—

<u>CASE</u>

Fuck these clowns, cuz. They want *Case One* out the hood?!

Case takes his *blue bandana* from his back-pocket and ties it around his face then reaches under his seat and grabs a 16 Shot 9 MM Beretta raising it in the air, releasing the chamber. BANG!

A gunshot echoes through the Bel Air canyons as Grant and the mob freeze, shitting themselves. Case has a look of pure hatred in his eyes, anything could happen now.

Case is very familiar with these situations, that gun he's holding is dirty as fuck. In fact he was supposed to drop it off the pier after they shot up some bloods from Culver City, he figured since it was already dirty, why not throw some more on it.

Maple and the girls are scared silent—

GRANT

Easy, dude... It was just a fight.

Case aims right at Grant, whose face is
pretty lumped up. Kids start running away and
girls scream, it is total pandemonium now. Den
is well battered, lying on the ground,
disoriented. Case and Blast also have some
meaty lumps, all of them bleeding badly.

Case suddenly notices his new shirt is all
torn up—

DEN

Case, it's cool, bro, chill.

CASE

Awww, my shirt?! What's up rich-boys? You
too cool, fool? Can't share the wealth?
Check me out, you like me?!

Everyone is nervous as hell as he
methodically aims the gun at them; Grant fears
for his life for the first time ever, his
buddies are scared blue as *Smurfette*.

Never in their short lives has anything like
this happened, they've always been the alpha-
males on the scene, bullying who they want,
talking girls into giving them hand-jobs to be
more popular, buying *cocaine* not *Meth*.

Case steps forward and the entire crowd
steps back—

CASE

You're better than me? 'Cause I don't
have money?! Jump us 'cause we come to
your big-ass mansion way up here by God.
You Moses on your mountain top? Huh?! How
'bout I cap your punk ass, rich-boy?

He aims at Grant, who cowers away—

GRANT

Be cool, man, please...

CASE

Now it's cool and please. First it's tough guy, now look.

Den pushes himself up, grabbing Case's shoulder firmly.

DEN

Let's just break, alright.

Case shrugs his hand away, inconsolably pissed off. Den matches eyes with Maple, her face is shocked-pale with fear and panic. Den is furious at himself that he was somehow the cause of it; another epic blow to his life makes him want to disappear under a rock.

Den then notices all the phones filming them, so many phones aimed at Case and his gun, this is fucking *real bad*.

CASE

I got nothing against you, rich-boy. I even got dressed up for this. I was here to have a good time, meet some ladies, have a drink, chill, then you trip?!

Jessica is on her phone, panicked—

JESSICA

I'M CALLING THE COPS!!!

                          TIFF

      If you call the cops they're totally
      going to break up your party. No one's
           dead, right? I mean, not yet.

      Blast yells out from inside the car as he
      squeezes into the backseat like a melon in a
      tennis can.

                          BLAST

           Case, let's go, man! Cops!

      Case slowly lowers the gun, backing away.

                          CASE

      For every mil you have in yo bank, I got
         nine mil in my chamber, cuz. This is
              Ghost Town Crips, nigga!

      Den and Case get in the car; it rumbles to
      life, hydraulics spit and it rises, 808
      bumping, metal frame rattling. He backs up and
      peals down the driveway, leaving a rubber burn
      on the pavement.

                          GRANT

           That guy is a dead-man.

      The crowd converges on Grant and his buddies
      sympathetically. Grant and the others glare at
      Maple accusingly. Maple starts shaking, all of
      this just a little too much for her to handle
      right now.

                          GRANT

      Hey, Maple, next time you want to bring
      your garbage to someone's house, don't.

Maple starts to break down, Carly and Tiff reach out to her but she runs to her BMW.

                    GRANT

    Run away, Maple! That's what you do best!
            Just like your mother!

Maple starts up her SUV and recklessly departs the scene, horribly shaken, upset in every way.

CASE'S VW BUG - NIGHT

The music blares, no one speaks. Den looks out the window, city passing by, face beaten up. Not even close to the first time he's been punched and kicked, he can't even recall the amount of times he's been jacked-up, this time it was different, it was embarrassing.

                    CASE

    Don't even trip, Den, I know where that
    bitch lives, we'll go back and get that
                chumps address—

                    DEN

    What the hell was that, Case?! A gun,
    bro?! You shot a gun? What're you
                thinking?!

                    CASE

    I'm thinking I'm saved your ass, those
    jocks were stomping you out, Den.

                    BLAST

    Forget about it, homies. We never should
                have gone.

                    CASE

    'Cause we're broke, dog? Nah, I go where
                I want.

DEN

Didn't you see them all filming? That shit is gonna be all over the internet, bro, this is fucking bad. I won't see it, but when this goes viral pigs will be sniffin', Case. They have it all on film!

BLAST

No way are we getting away with this.

CASE

Fuck it, least we go out famous, cuz. And I made a *dope-ass speech* to them cracka-ass-bitches.

DEN

It doesn't matter, none of this does, it's all bullsh—

CASE

Yo! Kill that, Den. We're as much a man as any of those punks. What? They got *luchi* so I have to bow down like a peasant, homie?

DEN

That's not what I mean… I just… I wanna *drive* to pick her up, take her to eat, chill, stuff, like that. I can't afford lunch for just me much less a girl like her. Ain't about her luchi, bro, so don't even think it. It's her, she's just—

CASE

Filthy-fucking-rich and you po-white-trash. Face it, they don't want us and we don't belong. We can't compete with what they're used to.

                    BLAST

I feel you there, I never feed outside my
zone. I stick with chicks that know broke
      like I know broke, very well.

                    CASE

That may be the deal, but yo, Maple sees
   in you what none of those idiots will
  ever have. Flavor, cuz. You're an artist,
  a rebel, a skater, surfer, you bomb the
hell outta LA, bro, trust me, you bombed
         the hell outta her mind too.

VENICE STREETS - NIGHT

   The streets are quiet until that 808 bass
bumps in the distance giving birth to Case's
car as it pulls to a stop in the borderlands
of Santa Monica and Venice Beach, hydraulics
spitting as it lowers to the ground. The door
opens and Den steps out, raising the seat for
Blast. Case turns down the music—

                    CASE

       Homies alright from here?

                    DEN

          We're cool. Thanks.

                    BLAST

    Yeah, Case, you saved our asses!

                    CASE

Sorry, I was trippin'. I didn't know what
              else to do.

                    BLAST

   Tripping?! That was bad-ass. They were
squirting themselves, dude, did you see
                them?!

Blast mimics Grant shitting himself,
laughing about it.

                    DEN

         It's not funny, man. That's not funny.
                 Don't do that!

Den grabs Blast, getting in his face—

                    DEN

         It's not a joke! You want someone dead?!
         You want to see someone with their brains
          blown out?! Is that cool to you?! You
         ever seen that?! You seen brains before?!

Den has tears welling in his eyes, Case
looks away, Blast is totally thrown off.

                    DEN

         It's not a joke! When people die, it's
         real, they die for good, forever. That
         was stupid Case! Gang-banger bullshit,
              bro! It's all on film?!

                    CASE

         I had colors on my face, cuz.

                    DEN

         What about your car? What about me and
         Blast? We could all go to jail for this!

                    CASE

                 Yo, cuz—

Den grabs his skate, dropping the wheels to
the concrete with a loud *slap*.

                    DEN

         Save that *cuz* shit for Ghost Town, Case.
           I don't want any part of it.

Den skates off, tormented by his impossible life as Blast reaches in the Bug grabbing his skateboard, also bummed out.

                         CASE

          He'll cool off. It's his brother, you
          know? He was there when it happened.

Case reaches over and shuts the door and Blast drops his skate to the concrete. Hydraulics spit, the VW raises and he peals out, heading back to Santa Monica. Blast looks down the street and can just see Den; he skates after his friend, very concerned.

VENICE STREETS - MOMENTS LATER

Den hauls ass, not slowing down for Blast who yells out for him to wait. Den pushes so fast he can't keep steady, skateboard hitting a large crack in the sidewalk, stopping.

Den flies off his skateboard and tumbles to a stop, moaning quietly with the discomfort of a rough landing. Pissed off, Den gets ups, grabs his skate and smashes it into a store window, *shattering the large panel of glass*.

Blast catches up—

                         BLAST

              Hey, man. Den—

                         DEN

          What do you want, Blast?! Fuckin' toy!
          Leave!

Den is seething now, terribly upset, every harsh memory, every frustration, every anxiety, and every loss flooding out of him, his hardened shell fighting back every last tear.

Blast steps to him, trying to comfort him, knowing Den has had a hard life, knowing his best friend needs him more than ever.

BLAST

I'm sorry—

DEN

LEAVE ME ALONE!

Den pushes him away, grabs his board and skates off. Blast realizes now isn't the time but never likes to see Den in pain, that's his bro, his road-dog, his homie.

BLAST

Come on, Den. Den!

Sirens sound in the distance; Blast looks toward the wailing nervously. He pulls a *Roark black Reload* with an *Astro-cap* out of his backpack, catching a monstrous UKA tag on the window beside the one Den shattered, brushy flares on each letter fat as cotton-candy.

He gets on his board and pushes down a side street, disappearing into the damp Venice Beach night.

MAPLE'S BEL AIR MANSION - SAME TIME

Maple pulls to a stop in front of her house, hands shaking, soul filled with angst. She gets out of her car and her knees nearly buckle but she gathers herself.

The house is big and empty, no one is home, no one is there for her, she is all alone in life and she's tired of it.

Maple slowly walks to the door, trying to put her key in the lock, hand shaking so bad she can't get it in.

She stops, sinks to her knees, and cries.

What the fuck is happening to her? How did all of this get set in motion? Is all of this her fault? Was that woman in the baseball hat her mother? Should she forget she ever met Den? What will she tell her father if Police come around asking questions?

Maple hadn't thought of the cops yet, but now what will she do? She had Den's phone number, she knows what school he goes to, what he does, who he is, what if cops ask about him? Will she lie?

Maple's father would kill her if he found out. This is all just too much right now; she breaks down.

BLAST'S HOUSE - LATER THAT NIGHT

Blast skates up to his pad, the party in full swing now, people everywhere, the street, front lawn, backyard, inside, outside, there are even several people on the roof. All types of people from surfers, to taggers, gang-bangers and stoners, nerds and hipsters, all walks of life come together in *Venice Beach*.

Blast kicks his board up and walks through the side gate into the backyard where it is controlled chaos, *sort of*. One thing is certain; there are some really wasted people here.

He makes his way through the crowd toward Fyre at the DJ stand, passing Casper, Sueno and a group of Cyclones by the keg. They don't notice him but Fyre immediately sees his battered face—

                        FYRE

          What the fuck, Blast?!

                       BLAST

      Got jumped at that party by thirty
             fuckin' jocks.

                        FYRE

              Where's Den?!

                       BLAST

    Don't know, he bailed after Case dropped
     us off. He got beat way worse than me.

                        FYRE

          By jocks?! What happened?!

                       BLAST

    Some *rich-dicks* at the party bum-rushed
      us out of nowhere, Case had to pull a
          strap, fuckin' shot at 'em, people
       screaming, running all over, filming us.

    Fyre drops her headphones and takes off out
of the party without another word. Blast sees
Casper watching her; dangerously curious about
where Fyre is headed.

    Casper matches eyes with Blast, expression
turning dark. He raises his hand to his
throat, slicing across his neck. Blast gulps
deeply, not liking where all of this is going.

                       RA-ONE

           What's up, homie?

    Blast turns to find Ra-one and Syne walking
up, bong in hand—

                        SYNE

          Dude, you got jacked up.

                              BLAST
             Yeah, shit got ugly real quick.

     Blast looks back over toward Casper only to
see him, Sueno, and several other C-13 heads
walking out of the party together in the same
direction as Fyre.

VENICE GRAFFITI WALLS - NIGHT

     The Venice Boardwalk is deathly quiet, only
people out are the homeless and the drug
addicted. Not a cloud in the sky, bright
moonlight washes over everything, making it
glow in a silvery hue.

     Den sits on the far side of the graffiti
walls, facing the crashing ocean, wind runs
it's invisible fingers through Den's thick
hair, his face swollen and bruised, dried
blood flaking off his cheeks and chin. All he
wanted to do was something different, to
experience something new, to know a different
world. What does that world do to him? Shits
all over him, just a heaving dump forcing him
back to the shit-hole he came from, back to
the unending poverty and never-ending
uncertainty. Whatever, right? What else is
new? Should have been expected.

     This has been the way life has gone since he
can remember; in fact he has not one memory of
smooth sailing at all. From the womb to the
trailer-park, that was his lot in life. God
what he would do to be a baby again, to not
recall anything from moment to moment, to be
fed and changed, cuddled and loved. Den was at
least sure that he was a happy baby, his
mother loved him so much there is no way she
wasn't an amazing mommy.

Den drops his head in his hands, holding back a wave of emotion.

Fyre steps from around the wall, energy radiant and strong, she looks down at Den bundled up, vulnerable and shattered. She sits beside him, not saying a word.

She has been in Den's life a long time and feels when he doesn't want to talk, knows he doesn't want her there. Inevitably something inside Fyre has always moved her in his direction no matter what.

Fyre knows she is jealous of Maple and actually cannot stand Casper or his gang-banger friends. Right now more than ever she wishes so badly she had never broke up with him, all Fyre can think about is laying safely in Den's arms. There was no better feeling than Den's arms. A cold truth she wouldn't recognize until months later waking up with Casper after hours of soul-degrading *Meth-sex* feeling like an empty shell; wanting to kill herself.

She never felt that way with Den—

                         FYRE

            Wanna go to my place?

FYRE'S BEDROOM - LATER

Fyre's bedroom is small and cluttered, only benefit to being in this old of a building is it's right off the boardwalk. Her walls are covered in tags and graffiti, clothes racks surround a messy double bed and clothes are everywhere. An empty area by the window is evidence of where she keeps her DJ set-up. Huge, brightly-colored Hindu-patterned drapery hangs from the ceiling giving the room a

Bedouin tent-like feel, other that, it's a
mess.

The door flies open, two ex-lovers fall into
the room, stripping clothes off, kissing
passionately, spilling onto the bed they get
to underwear when Den stops suddenly—

                    DEN

      Wait a minute... You and Casper.

                    FYRE

              So? Come on...

Den looks down at her; the pulsating city
lights play on her blushed-face, lips
quivering, hands clasping his hips, sliding
toward his waistband. He gets up—

                    DEN

      I can't do this. It's trouble. It's not
                  worth it.

                    FYRE

      What are you talking about? He'll never
              know. I won't tell.

                    DEN

      It's not even about him, Fyre. I'm just--
      What are we doing here? If we do this
      only bad will come of it. Horrible shit.

Den puts his pants on and throws his shirt
over his shoulder, grabbing his shoes and
skate—

                    FYRE

      Why are you tripping so hard...? Is it that
              rich-ho? She ain't that fine.

                          DEN

     She's not a ho, Fyre. This has absolutely
     nothing to do with her, I'll never see
     her again anyway, not after tonight, no
     fuckin' way. Plus Case shooting off his
     fucking gun, giving his *Scarface* speech
     is probably already on *Facebook*, *Youtube*,
     Instagram, *Vimeo*, you fuckin name it!

     Den slides on his paint covered shoes, the
     toe hole now much bigger from the stresses of
     the fight. He wiggles his toe out of the tear,
     whole life represented right there. He is
     about to open up to Fyre, gazing deeply at
     her, but stops himself. She isn't the one to
     share with anymore.

                          DEN

          Forget it. Never mind.

     Den heads out the door, not looking back.
     Fyer is shocked, nothing like this has ever
     happened to her before. She has never been
     rejected, she always does the rejecting. What
     the fuck is this?

     She steps over to her window and looks down
     at the street, expecting to see Den exiting
     the building.

                          FYER

          Oh shit.

     Up the block is Casper's Coupe De Ville,
     sitting in the shadows of another building.
     Fyer quickly puts her clothes back on, in a
     hurry to catch Den—

FYRE'S APARTMENT - NIGHT

A five story brick building grows from a sketchy street, built in the 1930's if this building could talk it would scream. Venice Boardwalk only a block away and down the sidewalk are rows of tents and homeless.

Den comes from the building, shirt thrown over his shoulder, bare-chested, skate in hand. He drops his skate to the sidewalk, slipping his shirt back on, distressed.

Den look at a homeless woman sleeping on cardboard, not even a tent to shelter her. All she has is a thin, tattered, dirty kids blanket with characters from *"The Rug Rats"* printed over it and a Dodgers baseball hat covering her face. To what end is this life headed? What's it all worth? How did he get here? Where the fuck is he going? Can he sign up for that scholarship USC is sponsoring? Maybe he could go to university?

He reaches in his pocket, taking his last three-dollars, he places it next to the woman.

Den steps on his skateboard and pushes off toward the boardwalk, in the opposite direction of Casper and C-13.

COUP DE VILLE - NIGHT

Casper and Sueno sit in the Coup de Ville, two other scary-ass cholos in the back, all watching Den roll out of view down the boardwalk. Casper puffs on a Meth pipe then passes it to Sueno.

CASPER

That bitch fuckin' my girl I'm-a smoke his ass, Sueno.

Casper is a second generation member of Cyclones 13, he was literally raised in the gang. His father used to slang Fyer's dad's dope, so did his step-mom and uncle for that matter. Then his three older brothers started slanging dope and got into the gang.

After his father went to jail for distribution of crack-cocaine and heroin, attempted murder, assault with a deadly weapon, fencing stolen goods, and a number of other charges, the four Fitzpatrick boys were on their own with their step-mother, who was more like a *Madame in a whorehouse of amphetamines*.

His father went to prison for a forty-six year bid; three months later Casper walked in on his oldest brother fucking their step-mom in the kitchen.

He wasn't even shocked.

Three days later his brother went to jail for stabbing a gas-station attendant when he refused to sell him beer after hours. Now it was just two older brothers. That's when Casper let his two older brothers jump him into C-13; this kid never had a chance.

Getting jumped into a gang usually consists of two or more members beating the shit out of a new prospect so he knows what it feels like to get fucked up while proving his toughness.

It's a *win-win* situation.

One moment he was known as Little Jimmy, an eleven year old pimple-face kid still wanting to build with Legos, the next he was *Casper* from *Cyclones 13 Pee-wee Locos*. Pee-wee Locos was for members fourteen and younger.

Three months after he got jumped into the gang, he walked in on his step-mom fucking his second oldest brother in the living-room. I should mention this is when the family crossed over into the *Meth* business and all were sniffing, smoking, or slamming it.

Meth use to scare the fuck out of Casper after his father tried to kill their family whilst on an eleven day bender. His father was convinced they had been possessed by the devil and needed to be cleansed in their own blood. Fortunately Casper's two oldest brothers were already in their late teens and rough as pit-bulls, they beat the shit out of their dad instead, putting him in the hospital.

His second oldest brother then got shot in the spine and head, now is an immobile-vegetable in their living room drooling, shitting, and pissing all over himself. They do their best to take care of him, he's still family and they love him. The only time they ever get a reaction out of him is when *Meth hits* are blown in his face causing him to rock wildly back and forth, groaning like a *Walrus*.

Casper hasn't walked in on his step-mom fucking his last brother yet, and even though his step-mom did hit on him one night, he hasn't fucked her either.

<u>CASPER</u>

I'm-a fuck up his entire world.

<u>FYRE'S VOICE</u>

Casper, what's up?

Casper comes out of his *Meth-daze* to find Fyre leaning in his window, concerned.

<u>CASPER</u>

Eh, what the fuck you doin' fuckin' with Den?! I just seen that faggot run off without his shirt on.

FYRE

I would never lie to you Casper. Den and Blast got jumped by some rich-fuckers at a party in the hills, he was really fucked up, I was only helping him clean up, I swear to god.

CASPER

Pussy-bitch getting' a beat-down by rich faggots don't mean shit. If I choose to believe you I still gotta fuck Den up.

FYER

Casper, Den's not a bad dude. His brother was in Ghost Town, he isn't. He *never* hangs out with 'em. That idiot Case was his brother's friend, not his.

SUENO

We'll have to at least sweat that *pendejo* a little, homie. Put some fear in 'im.

FYER

Whatever, just don't hurt him, ok?

CASPER

I'll think about it. Want a baggy.

By baggy he means Meth, which right now would suit Fyre fine, an escape from life would be welcome. She stops a moment, thinking about the outcome.

Fyre was certain that her mom, her dad, Den's mom, fuck near everyone's parent's she knew were still or used to be alcoholic-dope-heads. She was sure none of them thought they were going to ruin their lives partying. That's how it starts; a few years later you're twenty-five with three kids by two guys. *Fuck no*, that isn't going to be Fyre's story, not tonight anyway.

FYRE

Not tonight, Casper. See ya tomorrow.

Fyre walks off without even a kiss, but Casper don't care, he already tapped that ass, she can bounce if she wants. Sueno passes the Meth-pipe to Casper who takes out his torch and blazes it up.

DEN'S APARTMENT - NIGHT

Den's mother sleeps on the couch, TV till on playing an old re-run of *"Three's Company"*, Jack has himself in a comedic love-triangle once again. A near empty bottle of Smirnoff Vodka is on the table next to an over-flowing ashtray, cigarette butts spilling over, thin layer of smoke still settled in the air.

The door opens; Den steps in seeing his mother passed-out on the couch, vodka on the table.

Den shuts the door and walks to his mother draping a blanket over her, sitting close. He pets her gently, leaning down he kisses her on the head, not knowing what else to do. He takes the vodka and ashtray from the table, walking into their tiny kitchen to pour it out. He empties the thousand cigarette butts in the trash then holds the vodka over the sink, stopping as the first drop of alcohol falls from the lip of the bottle.

He looks at the vodka, it says to him, *"Drink me, for I am open. Drink me for I am soothing."*

Raising the medicine to his lips, Den watches the *elixir of life* roll slyly toward his tongue, oblivion but a sip away. Before the vodka touches his lips he moves his mouth,

allowing it to pour on the floor; *all of it.*
Den grabs a dish-towel, throws it in the
puddle then hurls the bottle across the room
busting a softball-size hole in the drywall
while shattering the bottle.

His mom doesn't even stir, completely passed
out. Must have popped a Xanax too he figures.
Their phone starts ringing, which is very odd.
Maybe it's Blast or Case checking on him? Or
Fyre? He stares at it for a long moment but it
won't stop ringing.

Finally, he answers—

DEN
Hello?

MAPLE'S BEDROOM - SAME TIME

Maple sits at her desk, cellphone to her
ear, still in her clothes from the party with
a half glass of white wine in her hand,
staring at Den's picture on her computer
monitor. Why she is calling him, she doesn't
know, she doesn't feel like there is anyone
else to call, no one that gets her anymore, or
no one that really wants to get her.

Maybe Den is the one who will get her—

MAPLE
Can I see you tomorrow...?

DEN'S APARTMENT - SAME TIME

Den can't believe his ears; he slumps
against the counter suddenly feeling whole
again, like there is hope again. When he left
Fyre's pad he had already decided nothing else
matters except making choices toward a better

future, Den accepted he would likely never hear from Maple again and was glad he never asked for her number.

DEN

    I'd like that, but I don't know. I mean, the cops are going to be looking for us.

MAPLE'S BEDROOM - SAME TIME

    Maple scrolls through the many pictures she has of Den at the beach, she loves them all, and him.

MAPLE

    Tiff called, my GF, she said cops only came to the bottom gate. Grant didn't tell about the gun, he said it was fireworks. Jessica didn't want her party broken up so went along with it. Grant said he lied because he doesn't want you in jail, since you'll be safe there. Guess he's planning some revenge plot. I won't tell him anything about you. I hate him, he's such a *dick-head*.

DEN'S APARTMENT - SAME TIME

    Den stares at his mom, her life, his life, this life, the mess that is this life. When will it change? Is it forever destined for trouble? He doesn't even like trouble. Sure, he enjoys vandalizing public and private property as often as possible, but that isn't causing trouble, that's *catching-fame*.

DEN

    Grant can do whatever, like I care. I came there to see you and you only.

DEN

Least fifty people got that whole thing
on film though. I may not *have* the
internet but I know what it is.

MAPLE'S BEDROOM - SAME TIME

Maple flops down on her bed holding a
freshly printed picture of Den, his brooding
good-looks suggest a rebellious nature. That
is the one thing Maple has never had;
rebellion.

She turns her speaker-phone on, sets it next
to her on the bed, holding the picture in
front of it, his voice coming from behind the
photo gives the illusion Den is in bed with
her, comforting her.

MAPLE

Grant is all talk anyway. I didn't think
about people filming, I was so upset and
scared I didn't even notice. I may be on
there too, I left right after you.

DEN'S VOICE

Guess we're in the same boat.

MAPLE

If this comes out, I'll probably never
see you again, at least not until I'm
eighteen, but whatever, I just want to at
least see you for as long as I can

DEN'S VOICE

Why do you want to see me? I'm a fuckin'
nobody who has nothing, from nowhere. Why
would you ever in a million years want to
see me?

DEN

My best friend shot off a gun at your
best friend's birthday party. I'd never
talk to me again.

MAPLE

I don't know... I just need to. Will you
see me?

DEN'S VOICE

I'd like that very much, Maple. I'm sorry
for everything. I was hoping to just hang
out with you, see what your world was all
about, you know? You're so different than
I am, so much more innocent than me.

Maple rolls over, lost in Den's eyes,
running fingers down his face.

MAPLE

Then I'll see you tomorrow. I can meet
you at the graffiti walls if you want.

DEN'S VOICE

I can be there by noon.

MAPLE

I'm so happy you're ok, Den.

DEN

Gnite Maple-like-the-syrup.

MAPLE

Goodnight Den-short-for-Dennis.

A smiling Maple ends the call, holding Den's
picture to her chest. For the first time in
her life she believes in the possibility of
what her mom always spoke of, *true love*.

CHAPTER EIGHT - BRIGHT DAY DAWNING
DEN'S APARTMENT - MORNING

A mid-morning sun bleaches the widows, radiating hope all over the now clean living-room. Den's mom is no longer on the couch but the hole is still in the wall. Den comes out of the kitchen with a plate of eggs, bacon, toast, and steaming cup of coffee on a waitress-tray.

Den pushes Connie's door open with his foot—

DEN

Up and at 'em, mom!

Connie is lying in bed, still in her clothes, feeling like shit. Den sets the tray down on the bed.

DEN

You should eat. Mom?

She stirs, groaning into consciousness.

CONNIE

Yyeeaahh. I'm up—

She rolls over, opening her puffy eyes, seeing Den's face for the first time. It's not as bad the morning after, he definitely has a nice black-eye and swollen-lip.

Connie sits up, worried—

CONNIE

What the hell? Den—

DEN

It's fine, mom. Just ran into a sizeable
social barrier.

CONNIE

What happened, baby?

Connie gently caresses his injured face; he
softly pushes away and gestures to her food.

DEN

Just-- Eat, take a shower, chill.
Everything will be alright. Fyre's mom is
coming by to take you to a meeting,
alright? You need to worry about you.

Den rises, she starts to protest but—

DEN

Eat, mom. Please? I gotta a hottie to
meet. I'm fine, I promise. I love you.

CONNIE

I love you too baby.

Mother and son share an emotional moment.
Life's been tough, but they'll make it, plus
she's way too hungover to ask any more
questions. Den walks out of her room, she
looks down at the wonderful breakfast he made
her, eyes welling up with tears.

Connie was raised in Sacramento by a mother
that was a quiet drunk and drunk-father that
was *verbally abusive and insane*. When she was
eighteen, her boyfriend convinced her to split
to Santa Cruz so she could watch him surf all

day. That was enough for her, she packed one duffel-bag and they left. Within three months she and her boyfriend were strung out on heroin and he only surfed once.

She went home with her tail between her legs, enduring another year of mother's drunkenness and a *glazed* father's ridicule.

"Connie, you're a whore, a loser, an idiot, a moron, you'll never amount to anything, you may as well die, get a life, get out!"

Connie started bartending at a biker-bar in South Sacramento and quickly moved in with a biker from a Motorcycle Club called, *"ROVING REBELS"*, one of Sacramento's oldest MC's dating back to the 1950's.

He wasn't a bad guy actually; in fact he really loved her. One year later Den's brother was born, three years after that Dennis was too. The pressure of a bigger family pushed his father to get involved in the more criminal activities the Rebels were involved in, eventually getting busted in city-wide Racketeering case brought against the MC; he went to jail for three years, a light sentence in comparison to most.

Den was only one year old. From what his brother says, these were the hardest years of their life. Connie moved back with her parents, her father was worse than ever, mother absolutely obliterated, skin yellowed with jaundice. In two-and-a-half years Den's dad was released and came to get her, moving them into a *Winnebago* parked in a club member's driveway.

The next year and change was one of constant fighting and drinking leading up to the night his father hit his mother for the first time. He hit her hard, *real hard*. It was an open handed slap but Den's dad was big and knocked her clean out.

The next morning, scared of his own actions, their dad moved to Winnipeg and joined a Canadian chapter of the *Roving Rebels, MC* and that was the last time he was ever seen or heard from again.

They stayed living in the Winnebago another eight months until Connie could figure something out, having at least sobered up, joining AA. A girlfriend she met there was moving to Venice Beach and offered to take Connie and her kids with her, even allowing them to live together until Connie was able to get her own place.

Those were the best times ever for Den and his brother, the time they had two moms. It only lasted about a year, Connie and she aren't even friends anymore, but that got them to Venice Beach, that laid the groundwork for every passing event up to this point, and as far as Den is concerned, he wouldn't change it for anything.

VENICE GRAFFITI WALLS - DAY

Some toys are already painting over the murals TUF and TBS did the day before, it's a savage culture in the graffiti game. A *"Toy"* is a tagger or graffiti artist that sucks at what they do, and the chumps spitting-paint on the wall today are most assuredly *toys*.

Maple watches them paint over amazing art with crappy, fat, garish letters suddenly understanding what Den meant by *gone forever*. She never thought of it that way before, isn't sure she *could* think of it that way. What if at the end of a long day of taking photos she erased the memory card and kept none of them?

People would think she was insane. That is no different than what Den is doing, spending so much time and energy on a true work of art that will never be seen again. This gives her a deeper insight into Den and makes her love him even more.

DEN

Where's your camera?

Maple turns to find Den standing there wearing a pair of his mom's sunglasses, lip puffed out and black eye peeking out from under her shades, jaw swollen. The sunglasses look like a cheap knock-off of the ones Jackie O' used to wear, black and gaudy with square-ish edges, really rather comical.

Maple gasps at his injuries then laughs when she sees the sunglasses. Den laughs too; it hurts, causing him to wince with each chuckle, this makes them laugh even more.

Maple regains her composure, truly concerned.

MAPLE

I'm sorry, I was laughing at those sunglasses, they are—

DEN

My mom's.

MAPLE

I hope so. How are you? Are you ok?

DEN

Not my first beat down.

She looks down at the ground, ashamed. He takes off the sunglasses to see her better.

Maple gasps at the true sight of his injuries.

                    MAPLE
        I am so sorry, Den. I didn't think-- I
        mean, Grant, I don't know. I'm just
                sorry, you know.

                    DEN
        Don't worry about it. Let's walk.

VENICE BEACH - LATER THAT DAY

   The sun levitates out over the great *royal-blue* Pacific, signaling a slow closure to the
day as sloppy waves crash on the shoreline,
seagulls wine, hopping about the beach in
search of food. The boardwalk waits in the
distance, painted in soft pastels and draped
by a salty-mist curtain.

   Maple and Den walk shoulder-to-shoulder up
the beach toward Santa Monica, but will never
get that far, not as slow as they're walking.
They don't want to be anywhere other than
right here.

                    MAPLE
        My mom got out of another rehab, which
            was her… fifth time, started using
        cocaine again almost right away, this
        time worse than ever. I don't know what
        she was trying to prove or escape from,
        she had everything. He forbade any drugs
            in the house, no pills, nothing. She
            would go out with her girlfriends and
            never come back. One time she was gone
            for ten days straight. I was so scared
            for her I couldn't sleep; I started
        pulling my own hair out. I had like, bald
            patches on a few places, it was so
            disgusting. I always wore a hat.

She got so bad my dad threatened to kick
her out, which is exactly what I think
she wanted anyway. That night she packed
like four suitcases, got in her car and
left. That was the last time I saw her.
She moved here to Venice to live with her
dealer, the jerk even came by our house
demanding money, my dad said they had no
divorce decree and didn't own her a dime.
He got a restraining order against them
both. She stopped calling me, then her
number disconnected. My dad used to tell
people she was dead, but she wasn't.

The thought of her mother being dead hits
her hard and tears well up, dripping hot down
her cheeks.

Den wants to put his arm around her but they
haven't even kissed, would it be weird?

He does nothing instead and just silently
listens, leaning into her a tiny bit, at least
bringing them closer.

MAPLE

I know she had to move out of that guy's
place six months later and my dad had her
car repossessed. I think she became
homeless after that. Once I got my
driver's license I started coming here to
find her, taking the photography elective
in school so I could have an excuse to
find her. It's stupid really, for all I
know she lives in Vegas, I don't know,
It's all just... very sad really.

DEN

Why didn't he save her? With that money—

144

MAPLE

Money makes it worse. She went through every rehab in town, never stopped her, just gave her a vacation from everything. Personally I think she would be happy permanently institutionalized, that's what she said it was like living with my dad, *"living in a mad-house"*. My dad can be kind of a cold-hearted-dick for sure, but he never hit her, rarely yelled at her, always tried supporting her to go back into law or find a passion, he would have paid for her to go back to school if she wanted. I kind of think she just wanted to go drink and do drugs. That's exactly what drove my father away from her; still it's all she kept doing in spite of losing it all.

DEN

I can understand. My whole family are a bunch of alcoholics and drug addicts, hell I went through rehab at fourteen just after I got out of Juvi, haven't drank or used since.

MAPLE

Fourteen? Wow, that's young.

A dark cloud settles over Den's thoughts, Maple sees this, taking his hand in hers, clutching it like her life depends on it. He welcomes the gesture, fighting back emotions.

DEN

I saw my brother shot to death when I was thirteen. He was from the gang my friend that shot the gun is from, Case? Ghost Town Crips, they're from Santa Monica.

DEN

Case use to live in Venice when we were younger, he was my brother's first friend. Case was already into graff and got my brother into it. My mom used to draw a lot when we were kids, me and my brother did too, we drew all the time, it was all we had. No TV, no video games or internet. Year later Case moved to Santa Monica, ended up jumped into GTC. My brother was still hanging out with him so he got jumped in too. Didn't know they had beef with Cyclones 13 here in Venice. My brother started getting jumped all the time, stabbed twice, head cracked open, our apartment got bricks thrown through windows, it was hell, especially for my mom. She was losing it, started drinking all the time. My brother dropped out of school and moved in with Case. He never visited 'cause it was too dangerous. My brother was no pussy either. When he moved out of Venice he spent every waking moment on revenge. Fucked up a lot of dudes, shit I won't even speak of. He became an animal, just wasn't himself anymore. People said he killed a guy from C-13, I know he didn't. C-13 put him on notice, started harassing me too. Fyre kept them from fucking with me too hard. Her dad was connected to those guys, major player in Venice for a long time. I had a birthday coming up, my mom didn't let me hang with my brother so we planned to meet near the border of Venice and Santa Monica at a Burger King. I skated there, waited all day. He showed up with a brand new black-book to draw in, bunch of pencils, markers, a few joints. We ate, hung out, it was great.

DEN

When we walked out of Burger King to the
bus stop, three cholos, all masked up and
shit, came out of an alley and shot him
in the head.

Den stops, the flood of memory collapsing
him to the sand, she drops down with him,
holding him in her arms and he suddenly starts
sobbing uncontrollably.

DEN

I saw his brains come out of his head...
then he fell face first on the ground,
crushing his teeth... his teeth... they flew
everywhere. I picked up all his teeth, I
knew he would need them, then I picked...

He collapses deeply into her arms—

DEN

I picked up some of his brain... I tried to
put it back in his head. It wasn't
supposed to be on the street, it should
be in his head, Maple...

She holds him like she will never ever let
go again, tears drench her cheeks which are
red with sadness.

MAPLE

It's ok, Den, I'm here for you.

Den slowly gets it together, controlling his
breathing.

DEN

I started using after that, weed, booze,
speed, whatever, anything to escape. I
was robbing people, breaking into houses,
shop-lifting, anything to get more. I got
busted so many times; they finally put me
in this state-sponsored rehab for six
months. Never looked back.

Den sits up, wiping his face carefully,
embarrassed as a nun in a strip-club. How did
two people from *polar opposite* worlds with so
much pain in common come together? Some
experiences transcend money and cars, houses
and zip codes, races and religions, cultures
and nationalities.

Certain experiences are universal, like pain
and loss, like love and hate. If any two
people on planet earth ever thought they found
love, these two are it.

MAPLE

I'm just... so lucky to know you, Den.

DEN

I'm lucky to know you, Maple.

The sound of drumming reverberates deeply
off the beach, tribal and haunting. Maple
looks around, curious if it is the sound of
her own heart or something else.

DEN

Never heard the drum circle? Pretty
amazing. Check it out?

He points in the distance where a group of
people crowd around in a circle, dozens of

different kinds of drums pounding away in a pulsing rhythm, magical and romantic.

                    MAPLE

    No... Let's sit here and listen. Okay?

Den stares at her, it's impossible—

                    DEN

                Sure.

Den leans in and they kiss, not just any kiss either. A kiss with lifetimes of journeys behind it, each one quickening in a never ending quest to kiss again. He pulls her closer; she wraps herself around him, finally running her fingers through his hair.

There is nothing written yet for how long this kiss will last or if it wall last at all. Almost two years left of high-school, then who knows where Maple will go to college, plus her father will never agree to her dating someone like Den, it is a true recipe for disaster.

But this kiss… this kiss may just have the power to outlast all of that, this love may be like the old fashioned kind where it becomes the most cherished and precious gift ever bestowed upon man.

Love and fire.

They part from their kiss, studying one another they submerge deeply into that deadly abyss that no man returns from. Den wraps his arm around Maple and she rests her beautiful head on his shoulder, sun tucked into the horizon like a child ready for bed.

                    MAPLE

    I never want this moment to end.

VENICE HIGH ARTS CLASS - DAY

Class is well in session, students quietly work on their projects as Mrs. Morrison walks around examining the kids' progress; their work ever impressive.

Den sits by the window in dreamland, face still battered, *smushed-head sculpture* in front of him. Somewhere outside that room is his future lying in wait, a real future. Den can see it now, clear as the day is long, he can see it.

If he works hard, makes right choices, stays focused, lives a clean life, he can create his own way out of this never-ending cycle of poverty and disappointment.

Den is the key, Den is the secret, Den is the answer, Den and no-one else.

He comes out of his distraction when a group of kids beside him crowd around a phones watching something.

Den can just hear it a little, it sounds familiar. He eases over to them and looks down at the phone, sure as shit it's a video of Case's *Scarface* speech on *Youtube*.

MRS. MORRISON

I want those reports on *Cubism* by Friday. Those still interested in entering the scholarship competition; please see me at the end of class.

Den sits back at his table, newly stressed out. He takes out the photos Maple gave him and flips to the one of him with sunglasses on, in the reflection of the lenses he can see twin mirror images of Maple's perfect smile, rest of her face hidden behind a camera. He

runs his fingers across the image, still
tasting her lips, still catching the sweet
scent of vanilla in her hair.

This life isn't over, it's just beginning.

The school bell rings loud, snapping him out
of his stupor. He gathers his belongings, puts
his sculpture on a shelf, then heads toward
the door, but instead of leaving he walks to
his teacher.

                    DEN

        Mrs. Morrison? I want to enter the
                competition.

STREETS OF VENICE - MORNING

A few blocks from Venice High, Den and Blast
walk along the street, holding their
skateboards and talking excitedly. Teens
headed home from school excitedly walk, bike,
and skateboard along.

                   BLAST

        Can't believe it's already all over the
        net, dog. Case is pointing a gun, cops
                are gonna be on this.

                    DEN

        No one has video of the gun-shot. I went
        to the computer-lab after Art, scoured
        that shit, found like eighteen videos
        posted to different platforms, none show
        me, only thing of you is your fat ass
             squeezing in the back-seat.

                   BLAST

    Don't know how you're so calm about this.

                              DEN

        Because there's something bigger here, I
        can see light at the end of the drain-
        pipe. I'm gonna enter *and* win that USC
        art scholarship, Blast. Watch me.

                             BLAST

              Fuck yeah you are, homie.

                              DEN

          Can you imagine, Blast? Me in college?

                             BLAST

           That's so cool. I could totally imagine.

                              DEN

                  Why don't you enter?

                             BLAST

          I'm not in art class and grades are shit.

                              DEN

                  Oh, yeah. True.

                             BLAST

          Don't worry. We'll be friends while
          you're at USC. I'll be your starving
          artist roommate that seduces all the
                  freshman girls.

        They hear an 808 bass thump and rattle of a
        metal frame.

                             BLAST

                  Fuck, we're dead.

        Casper's Coup de Ville drives past and hangs
        a U-turn.

                              DEN

                  Just keep walking.

<u>BLAST</u>

We should run.

<u>DEN</u>

Don't be scared.

The Coup de Ville skids up the curb, music
bumping as Casper jumps out, pulling a knife—

<u>CASPER</u>

Think you can fuck my girl, bitch?

<u>DEN</u>

I didn't sleep with her, Casper.

<u>CASPER</u>

I saw you leave her crib, fool! I saw
you. I should stab you right here, Den.
Want that?!

<u>DEN</u>

Go ahead. Do it, I don't care.

Den raises his shirt exposing his stomach—

<u>DEN</u>

Come on Casper, stab me! Bring it! Do it!

Casper can't believe what he is witnessing
as Den grabs his hand, forcing the knife
toward his own belly.

<u>DEN</u>

Put it in me, Casper, stab me!

Casper looks around; a lot of witnesses,
least a dozen kids plus busy after-school
traffic. He yanks his hand away, shoving Den—

                    CASPER

        You *crazy*, homes. I ain't doin' time for
                    no punk ass.

                      DEN

          That's right... You're not.

    Sueno yells from the car, nervous as hell
    about all the people watching them.

                     SUENO

        Let's roll ese, fuck this *puto*.

    Casper backs toward his car, keeping his
    tough guy persona up.

                    CASPER

          Some other time then, bitch.

    Casper gets in his car and the Coup de Ville
    peels out in a cloud of smoke, burnt rubber,
    and deep bass.

                     BLAST

            That was bananas, dude.

                      DEN

        Whatever, so he kills me, big deal, I'll
        catch a heaven on the Pearly Gates when I
                    get there.

    Blast looks at Den, shocked. Den smiles and
    they walk off leaving bystanders speechless.

                     BLAST

        When did you hook up with Fyre?

DEN

I didn't, Blast. He thinks I did because
he's an idiot.

BLAST

Seemed pretty convinced to me.

DEN

None of this happening right now matters,
bro. I mean, I don't have words for it
but my brain tells me this shit doesn't
mean anything, none of it. Only thing
that does matter is the future. No one
can take that away from us, that's why I
ain't afraid of Casper or C-13. They
can't kill someone who ain't afraid to
die, and I ain't, future or no future.

BLAST

Riiiiight, if you weren't sober I'd ask
what you're smokin', cause you high, dog.

They reach the end of the block as the sound
of an 808 bass and metallic rattle causes
Blast to crap his diaper. They turn to see
Case pulling up in his Prince-purple VW,
turning down the music.

DEN

Case, shouldn't be here, C-13's all over.

BLAST

Casper just pulled a blade on Den,
fuckin' loco!

Hydraulics spit, car lowers and Case gets
out.

CASE

Fuck them wetbacks, cuz.

BLAST

I'm-a wetback. Casper's white as a ghost.

CASE

Then fuck that cracker, cuz.

DEN

I'm-a cracker, Case.

CASE

Then fuck you niggas, cuz. Got all my
bases covered now?

They laugh and huddle, friends forever.

CASE

I'm sorry, homies. I put you both in a
real fucked up position, I mean the
situation was real fucked up, but I had a
bat too. Won't put you out there like
that ever again, cool?

Den gives him the 'all good' shrug.

CASE

We still the Un-Known Artists?

DEN

Always the *Un-Known*, always the *artists*.

Den smirks and they get in Case's *Prince-
purple VW Bug*.

BLAST

UKA for life, my dudes!

DEN

You know you're famous, right?

CASE

Hell yeah, dog, one on *Youtube* already
got sixty-thousand views. Threw the hood
up and everything, homie. My dogs from
the pound think I am the fuckin man, cuz,
it's hilarious. Someone said they saw
that shit on local news, won't be long
before I get busted in my whip so let's
enjoy it.

Hydraulics spit, car raises, 808 bass kicks
and metal rattles as they peal out in a cloud
of smoke and burnt rubber, kids waving the
toxic fumes away with their hands, coughing.

DEN'S BEDROOM - NIGHT

Den has his head phones on, hip-hop bumping,
air brushing a new painting for art-class on a
large canvas. He sprays a blaze of colors,
sleek lines, abstract details, Den is in the
zone.

He stops spraying, sets his airbrush on its'
cradle, then steps away to take it in. The
near finished painting is of Maple reflected
in his sunglasses, only surreal and abstract,
image warped and elongated.

In this painting Maple doesn't have her
camera, just her beautiful face and perfect
smile. Behind her are the Venice Graffiti
Walls with her name Maple painted in Den's new
lettering style.

Den nods to the rhythm in his ears then
returns to his creation, bringing it to life.
Working toward a better future, for himself,
for his mother, for his friends, but most of
all... for a *drop-dead-gorgeous* girl named
Maple, you know...like the syrup?

IS THERE AN END?

Start writing one here...

NEVER ENDING